A THOROUGHLY COMPROMISED LADY

Bronwyn Scott

First published in Great Britain 2010
Harlequin Mills & Boon Limited,
Eton House, 18-24 Paradise Road, Richmond, Surrey TW9 1SR

© Nikki Poppen 2010

ISBN: 978 0 263 87598 0

Harlequin Mills & Boon policy is to use papers that are natural, renewable and recyclable products and made from wood grown in sustainable forests. The logging and manufacturing process conform to the legal environmental regulations of the country of origin.

Printed and bound in Spain
by Litografia Rosés, S.A., Barcelona

Bronwyn Scott is a communications instructor at Pierce College in the United States, and is the proud mother of three wonderful children (one boy and two girls). When she's not teaching or writing, she enjoys playing the piano, travelling—especially to Florence, Italy—and studying history and foreign languages.

Readers can stay in touch on Bronwyn's website, www.bronwynnscott.com, or at her blog, www.bronwynswriting.blogspot.com—she loves to hear from readers.

Recent novels from Bronwyn Scott:

PICKPOCKET COUNTESS
NOTORIOUS RAKE, INNOCENT LADY
THE VISCOUNT CLAIMS HIS BRIDE
THE EARL'S FORBIDDEN WARD
UNTAMED ROGUE, SCANDALOUS MISTRESS

and in Mills & Boon® Historical eBook *Undone!*

LIBERTINE LORD, PICKPOCKET MISS
PLEASURED BY THE ENGLISH SPY

For Wendi,
thanks for your support of the Brenda Novak auction
to raise funds for research in the fight against juvenile
diabetes. Your contribution makes all the difference.

For my family and friends
who are all so supportive of my writing,
especially the kiddos, Ro, Catie
and Brony, who let their mom write.
And for my editor, Joanne, too,
who worked extraordinarily hard
to make this story just right!

Chapter One

London—spring 1835

Jack Hanley, the first Viscount Wainsbridge, firmly believed that ballrooms were for business. Chandeliers, potted palms, sparkling champagne—all the standard trappings of festivity aside, ballrooms were a gentleman's office. They were the places a gentleman conducted the most important business transactions of his life: ensuring a place in society and arranging his marriage. Jack had already done the former and had no intentions of doing the latter. Tonight was no exception.

Jack stopped inside the arched entrance of the Fotheringay ballroom, halting a moment to adjust the sleeve of his evening jacket and surreptitiously scan the room. He took mental roll of the attendees. For all intents and purposes, it was an assembly of the usual suspects. That suited him well. This evening, his business was with the newly arrived Venezuelan delegation.

He had very specific orders to meet them, and determine if there was any substance to the quietly circulating rumours that Venezuela was spoiling for a fight over undeclared borders with British Guiana.

'Wainsbridge!' An excited female voice broke over the dull din of constant conversation. His hostess bore down upon him with a gaggle of females in tow. Jack swallowed a groan. The horde was descending slightly earlier than anticipated. That was the price of being a newly titled, attractive bachelor with a certain reputation with the ladies. It didn't help that he was still something of a novelty since his work for the Crown seldom brought him to London on a regular basis.

'Lady Fotheringay, how charming you look tonight.' Jack pasted on a benign smile that hid his cynicism. Women in ballrooms had their business too.

'I want you to meet my nieces, Wainsbridge.' The purple ostrich plumes in Lady Fotheringay's hair bobbed dangerously. There were five of them, all named after flowers—nieces, that was, not ostrich plumes, although he wouldn't put it past the silly woman to name them too.

By the time introductions were completed, Jack's court had grown substantially, filled with females clamouring for their hostess to introduce them to the handsome, newly minted viscount with the mysterious antecedents. For the moment he was hemmed in on all sides and not another man in sight. He could only guess where his fellow males had taken themselves off to— cards and the good brandy, no doubt.

Jack was listening with feigned interest to Miss Violet Fotheringay's rather unenlightened dissertation on the year's fashions and contemplating how he might extract himself from his group in order to find the Venezuelan delegation when he heard it: the unmistakable whisky-and-smoke sound of Lady Dulcinea Wycroft's laughter.

Even in a crush such as this, the sound was distinctive in a pleasant, provocative way, something akin to Odysseus's sirens; a sound that would make a smart man fear for his bachelor status. Of course, that assumed the woman in question wanted to marry at all. Dulcinea had shown no inclination in the eight years she'd been out to want to give up her reign as London's supreme Incomparable, although there had been many chances to do so—six proposals Jack knew about and probably a string of others he'd missed in his long and varied absences from town.

Such a resistance to matrimony made her all the more delightful in Jack's opinion. If there was one temptation Jack could not quite resist, it was a witty, cleverly spoken woman who was apparently as staunchly committed to remaining unmarried as he was.

Such a similarity made her a complex creature who was both potential companion and challenge. He loved nothing more than a good challenge and over the years, Dulcinea Wycroft had certainly proven to be that to the good men of the *ton*, none of whom yet had succeeded in walking her down the aisle, although it wasn't for lack of trying.

With careful eyes, so as not to neglect Miss Fotheringay,

Jack followed the laughter to its source. Ah, that explained where the men were. His was not the only court. Two pillars down the ballroom, Miss Wycroft reigned at her court of wit and beauty, surrounded by the cream of London's bachelors. This evening, gowned in striking pomegranate silk, the sheen of her impossibly blue-black hair catching the light of chandeliers, she was a veritable Helen of Troy.

Jack was not immune.

Neither was most of male London.

She was besieged with admirers. If he was the *ton*'s bachelor of note, she was the female equivalent. Like him, she'd not be conquered easily and certainly not by that gathering of pups. Jack stifled a smirk of superiority at the sight of the men clustered about her. The fools. Didn't they know they hadn't a chance? They were insignificant moths to her all-consuming flame. And really, who could blame them? She was vivacity personified in a room full of pattern-card women like Violet Fotheringay, all playing their assigned roles in life.

Those admirers would fare no better against her fire than the unlucky moth fared against the light. She would burn their ambitions as assuredly as she'd burned the would-be suitors that preceded them. A woman like Dulcinea would never settle for a typical *ton*nish marriage. Such a passion for living could not be caged inside a Mayfair mansion. Jack privately marvelled that such passion hadn't ruined her already. It was his experience in general that the brightest flames often consumed themselves. It was perhaps inevitable that

Dulci's fire would be her eventual downfall. Jack thought it rather miraculous it hadn't happened already.

He turned his gaze back to Violet, but his thoughts remained firmly elsewhere in the mental vicinity of Dulcinea. As a long-time friend of her brother Brandon, the earl, he'd known Dulci vaguely through the years although he hadn't known her well. He'd been filling various diplomatic posts in the Caribbean and had only just returned to England four years ago. It had been something of a surprise to return and encounter, on his brief appearances in London society, the incarnation of the current Dulci Wycroft. Breathtaking, too—not only in beauty, he discovered, but also in wit.

When he was in town, they ran in similar circles and were inevitably in attendance at the same dinner parties and political functions, not to mention larger events. This past winter, when his schedule had allowed him to remain in town, he'd found himself enjoying the exchange of verbal ripostes with her on several occasions.

Jack's thoughts paused and took another path. During the Christmas holidays, they'd exchanged more than ripostes, spurred on perhaps by the mistletoe and holiday spirits—he meant that literally. He'd kissed her in Lady Weatherby's orangery. Those kisses had unleashed something raw and dangerous between them.

Normally, such an attraction would lead to its natural conclusion where Jack was concerned. But Dulci superseded such logic and placed him in a double bind; the secretive and private nature of his work precluded the opportunity to pursue any kind of relationship—not that he was desirous of anything permanent, which led to the second bind. The relationship he would most likely pursue would hardly meet with Brandon's approval. One did not make a mistress of or have an affair with one's best friend's sister. And Jack wasn't about to marry her over a few wassail-driven kisses no one knew about.

Lord knew *that* particular encounter might have ended better—or worse, depending on how one looked at it—if he hadn't been unexpectedly summoned away from the house party. As it was, he'd been lucky to escape with only one pot being thrown at his head. Dulci had been furious over what she saw as his imposition, although Jack suspected she'd enjoyed the kiss just as much as he had. She wasn't angry with him. She was angry with herself.

The result was that these days their banter had taken on a slight edge. No matter. One look at her tonight and his body was perfectly willing to pick up where they'd left off, pottery shards and all.

So was every other man in the room. By rights, Dulci should have picked one of them by now and settled down to life as a society matron. But Dulci didn't do anything by the rules. She made no secret of her independence, of her enormous interest in the Royal Geographic Society and fencing, and that she enjoyed far more freedom than other unmarried women of good families. Such confidence in her own consequence was an enormous part of her appeal. No gentleman ever assumed for long that Dulci Wycroft *needed* a man to rely on.

She got away with it and much else, Jack knew,

because she was very careful not to break the one rule that mattered most. There was no blemish on her name in terms of maidenly modesty. Whatever wild streak Dulci might possess in conjunction with her independence, it did not extend into the realm of sexual exploits.

Jack thought of the orangery and reorganised his thoughts. Well, at least not beyond a few stolen kisses.

Not far down the room, Dulci leaned forwards, showing great signs of interest in the man on her left—and a considerable amount of bosom, in Jack's opinion. The man was a strikingly handsome Spaniard. Jack swore silently. Damn and double damn. He would have to go through her to get to them. With the episode in the orangery still between them, he'd have preferred to keep his business and pleasure separate.

He should have known. It stood to reason she'd be in the centre of the excitement. Dulci knew everyone in society. Those she didn't know, she made a point to meet. The delegation had only been in town a short week and Dulci had already managed to meet the guests of honour, the very people he'd come to investigate. According to the descriptions Jack had been provided with, the man at her side adroitly ogling her bosom was none other than Calisto Ortiz, one of the Venezuelan delegation, nephew to a high-ranking government official with ambitions. No doubt the others were somewhere in the crowd around her. He'd definitely have to get through Dulci to get an introduction. That meant there'd be a scene, at least a small one.

Considering their last words in the orangery, it was

to be expected. In truth, it was Dulci's due. He'd behaved badly. One did not steal kisses and then have to dash off in the middle of stealing a bit more.

Jack was suddenly aware that Miss Fotheringay had stopped talking. 'Quite insightful,' Jack said quickly, smiling at the young woman who looked at him expectantly. 'I am positive many young girls share your opinion.' He was sure they did, although he couldn't recall what those opinions might be. It was deuced awkward to be caught out with one's attentions fixed elsewhere. Time to be moving on.

'I have enjoyed this immensely, ladies, but I see some people I need to meet, if you would excuse me?' Jack moved smoothly through his court and discreetly headed towards the group around Dulcinea. He took the long route, careful not to hurt anyone's feelings. It wouldn't do to be immediately seen going from one set to another.

Jack tugged on his waistcoat, girding himself for battle. When he was with her, everything was a competition—a delightful competition, but still a competition—and he had to be ready. 'Steady on, old chap.' Jack muttered under his breath. He had nothing to fear. What fire didn't burn it made stronger. When it came to women like Dulci Wycroft, Jack was tempered Damascus steel.

Jack circumspectly dislodged a young admirer whose only crime was to stand next to Dulcinea. Good lord, the ring of admirers got younger by the year. Lord Baden's son was among the lot tonight. Was the boy really old enough to come up to town now? These men were barely men at all, merely overgrown pups. Or was it simply that he was getting older? At four and thirty, he felt quite the veteran standing amongst Dulci's collection of young bucks. Regardless, they were no match for Dulci's wit. Not one of them had a chance of holding her attention.

'Good evening, everyone.' His eyes briefly swept the group by way of greeting.

The group's collective eye fixed on him, their collective breath held, waiting for the sport to begin. It had become something of a ballroom sport for guests to watch Dulci and he spar. Well, sparring wasn't quite accurate. They didn't fight. They *volleyed* with dares and words carefully wrapped in a socially acceptable package. Jack preferred to classify their exchanges more along the lines of lawn tennis. With practiced charm he drawled, 'Good evening, Lady Dulcinea.'

The match was engaged.

Heads swivelled to Dulci. If she was surprised by his presence, she did not show it. Her greeting was coolly polite, the type one offered to a passing acquaintance although they were far more than that.

'Wainsbridge, I did not expect to see you tonight.' Dulci subjected him to a liquid blue perusal, taking in every inch of his attire.

Jack readied for the forthcoming quip. Amid her sea of dandies with their bright waistcoats and popinjay fashions, his sombre apparel, broken only by the dove-grey brocade of his waistcoat, took on a more austere cast. The king's prized adviser could not strut around looking like a peacock of the most frivolous order. Although what he advised the king on remained a mystery to many.

'Wainsbridge, are these gloomy tones the best you can do? Such a choice would put a damper on even the most festive of occasions.' Dulci quizzed him with a perfectly arched black eyebrow. Heads turned back to him, everyone considering his apparel.

Jack bowed, taking the reprimand with consummate ease. 'I am at your disposal, Lady Dulcinea. What colour would you prefer I wear? The rainbow is yours. Pluck a colour from it and I will see it done. By this time tomorrow, I shall possess apparel done up to your satisfaction.'

The group stared at Dulci, waiting for her pronouncement. Jack thought it highly likely he wouldn't be the only person sporting Dulci's colours by this time tomorrow. Tailors all over the city would be busy in the morning.

Dulci snapped open her fan and speared Jack with a knowing look. As he intended, she understood entirely the dilemma he'd placed before her. She could not dare him to wear a hideous colour without making her court appear ridiculous along with him. Nor could she take the uncreative neutral option since she'd been the one to throw down the gauntlet. She had a certain reputation to uphold just as much as he.

'Azure. I choose azure,' she announced coyly over the top of her painted fan after pretending to give the answer a great deal of thought. And perhaps she had. Jack had to admit blue was the perfect choice for a careful answer. There were so many shades of blue; a gentleman could pick a hue of his own comfort level.

Jack bowed again. 'Azure it shall be, Lady Dulcinea. I duly accept your charge with all these gentlemen as my witnesses. Tomorrow night, at the Danby rout, I shall carry out my commission.'

Jack turned his gaze to the man next to him in the circle as if noticing the Spanish gentleman for the first time. 'Lady Dulcinea, I must beg an introduction. I believe this gentleman and I are not acquainted.' The match was over. Dulci had won the dare, but he'd got what he came for. The rest of the group wouldn't realise that. But Dulci would.

Dulci gave a deceptively sweet smile and made the introductions. 'Wainsbridge, this is Señor Calisto Ortiz, of the Venezuelan diplomatic delegation. I had the good fortune to meet him at a Royal Geographic Society dinner a few days ago. *Señor*, allow me to present Viscount Wainsbridge.'

The Spaniard bowed smoothly and introduced two other gentlemen in turn, a Señor Adalberto Vargas, who was clearly the august leader of the delegation, and Señor Dias, whose mediocre clothing clearly marked him as the hanger-on.

Ortiz was all handsome manners and Jack disliked him immediately. Younger than his Venezuelan counterparts by over a decade, darkly handsome with inky hair, and expensively dressed, Calisto Ortiz radiated a rather obvious appeal of the kind women found charming. He did not endear himself to Jack further when he turned that charm on Dulci.

For tonight, he'd tolerated enough of the man's covert ogling of Dulci's bosom, as deliciously displayed as it was in the tight bodice of her gown. Like recognised like, and Jack recognised Ortiz to be a womaniser of the highest order.

It was time to throw down the gauntlet, in the politest of fashions, of course. A little competition always brought one's true colours to light and he did not expect Ortiz to prove the exception to the rule. Instead he fully expected Ortiz to prickle in response to a few well-placed remarks. It wasn't Jack's job to make friends. His orders were very clear: take the measure of the delegation. There wasn't a single word mentioned about befriending them.

Jack inserted himself into the general conversation during a lull, casually launching his first sally. 'Señor Ortiz, *como le gusta Londres*?'

His fluent command of the language had the desired effect. Ortiz looked momentarily surprised at hearing Spanish. Jack wanted him to be surprised and warned. The Venezuelans might be thousands of miles from home and those who knew the territory, but the English were not without their resources here. The Venezuelans would not be dealing with London-based politicians ignorant of the New World's geography.

Ortiz favoured him with a cold smile. 'I assure you my English is quite fluent.' His terse answer imbued a level of tension into the group. Touchy young man, Jack thought, to be so thoroughly insulted on the acquaintance of six words.

'Je parle français, aussi,' Ortiz went on, his steely gaze fixed intently on Jack.

'Très bien. J'aime parler français,' Jack smoothly switched into French. He could play this game for a while if Ortiz was so inclined. He might not have the formal degrees of a polyglot scholar, but Jack could bed a woman in six different languages.

Señor Vargas intervened swiftly. 'Señor Ortiz has been educated at the finest of schools. He's the nephew of one of the viceroys posted to our region.'

'Ah,' Jack exclaimed with all the appreciation he could summon. Señor Ortiz's role in the delegation was becoming clearer. 'Are you considered to hold an official diplomatic post, then?'

His enquiry hit the mark. It was petty gratification to see the handsome man's smile fade into a grim line. 'I'm an ombudsman.'

'I see. That's quite an impressive *title*.' Jack's steely tone conveyed the rest of the message to Ortiz. They both knew an ombudsman operated in a limited capacity. The title was honorary at best, a sop to one's ego.

Ortiz's dark eyes flashed dangerously. Jack answered with a cool smile. The man fully understood his allusion and had the good grace to be insulted. But the flare in his eyes suggested he did not have the good grace to be defeated. Ortiz would bear watching. His temper suggested he was a man quick to anger, quick to take impulsive actions that might later be regretted.

Dulci placed a hand on Jack's sleeve. 'It is time for that dance you promised me.'

Jack gave her easy compliance. There was no more to be gained from provoking Ortiz. He'd got what he came for. He'd taken the measure of the delegation and it was quite telling.

Chapter Two

Dulci's announcement was immediately unpopular with everyone except Jack. 'But the next waltz is mine,' a rather dull-witted fellow, the Earl of Carstairs's son, stepped forwards to protest.

The boy was not fast enough. Jack claimed indisputable possession, covering Dulci's gloved hand on his sleeve with his own. 'I'm sure Lady Dulcinea has something saved for you later.'

'I have a country dance free in the fourth set.' Dulci quickly offset the boy's sour face.

'Good choice,' Jack remarked in low tones, leading her towards the dance floor. 'Less conversational opportunities with a country dance. You're probably doing him a favour. I doubt he has the requisite half-hour of conversation saved up to get through a waltz.'

'I'm doing myself a favour.' Dulci placed her hand on Jack's shoulder as they positioned themselves. 'The man's got the brains and build of an ox. He stepped on my feet no less than five times last week at the Balfour ball.'

'Here I thought you were protecting Ortiz when in reality you were angling for a dance with me.'

'Don't flatter yourself. I'm not desperate to dance with you like the other women in the ballroom.'

'They want more than dancing from me, I assure you. You noticed my following? It is quite considerable.'

Dulci blushed as he intended.

'What? There's nothing wrong with the words "following" or "considerable".' Jack feigned ignorance of his innuendo.

'Except when *you* say them. I can't say I have noticed your "following", but I've noticed you're still as conceited as I remember in the orangery.'

Jack laughed at Dulci's pique, the familiar longings starting to stir. He was enjoying this: his hand at her back, the warmth of her body through the thin silk of her gown, his mind taking pleasure in the mental exercise of parrying her comments.

'It's the truth.' Jack swung them into the opening patterns of the waltz. He was starting to wonder if his emotional distance could be challenged tonight. He'd like nothing more than to try his luck at stealing a few kisses.

'That all women are dying of love for you?'

'No need to be envious. It's not as if you don't have the other half of London at your feet.' Jack shot a look at the jilted heir on the sidelines. 'I would have thought women found him rather handsome. He's tall, muscular in a beefy sort of way. Quite the pride of English manhood.'

'It will all run to fat in ten years,' Dulci said matter of factly. 'I prefer a leaner sort of man. Big men don't tend to dance well.'

'Your brother's tall,' Jack argued for the sake of disagreement. With Dulci, anything was fair game for an argument. 'The ladies love dancing with him whenever Nora gives them a chance.'

'Brandon's an exception.'

'Speaking of Brandon, I had a note from your brother a month ago. He and Nora are doing well.' Brandon was the one safe topic of conversation they had between them. 'I gathered they aren't coming up to town because of the new baby.'

'No, they won't be coming up. It's to be expected. They are the most doting of parents.' A small smile played across Dulci's lips at the mention of her new nephew, giving her features a rare soft look. It occurred to Jack that Dulci's long-standing reign as an Incomparable might indeed be a lonely one. The girlfriends who had débuted with her eight years ago would have long since married and started their own families. He had not thought of it in that way before—a price to be paid for her determination to remain unattached. Much in the same way he paid for the lifestyle he achieved. It had been quite unintentional on his part. Was that true for her as well?

It was also a stark reminder that he didn't know Dulci Wycroft all that well, all the ways she'd changed in the years of his absence. She'd come of age and entered society while he'd been off performing the various commissions that had eventually landed him his viscountcy.

Much of his adult life had been spent away from England doing things for the empire he couldn't share with another. The result was that he knew very little about the woman she'd become. Good God, when he'd left England she'd been sixteen, and he a mere twenty-four. Those intervening years were a blank. He knew only that her beauty, her wit, her innate fire for life and the wild side she strove to keep hidden drew him irrevocably despite his better intentions. Jack didn't dare contemplate too deeply the reasons for his inexplicable attraction. Those reasons were best left unexplored for fear of uncovering longings and truths that couldn't be answered or tolerated. He could not afford to fall in love with anyone, especially not Dulci. He'd have a hard time explaining that to Brandon.

Dulci cocked her head, studying him with her sharp gaze. 'What are you up to tonight, Jack? It must be important if it meant seeking me out. For the record, I was not fooled about your reasons for approaching me. You wanted that introduction.'

Jack executed a tight turn to avoid a collision with the less observant Earl of Hertfordshire. 'Do I have to be up to anything? Perhaps I just wanted to dance with the loveliest girl in the room?'

'Doubtful. The last time you saw me, I broke a pottery bowl over your head.' Dulci's eyes narrowed in speculation. 'You won't tell me what you're really doing here, will you?' she accused.

This was old ground. Old ground, old wound. It went beyond the quarrel in the orangery. He'd had this discussion before with other women. He was not at liberty to discuss his business with her or with anyone else. It was rather ironic that while achieving a title had made him socially acceptable and available, he was not at liberty to act on that availability. A woman was only entitled to part of him. The Crown got the other part without question or consideration.

Such a condition was not acceptable with Dulci. Her unattached status was proof of that. If she tolerated half-measures, she would have settled for a convenient *ton*nish marriage by now. But half-measures were all he could give. What he did for the king was of the utmost secrecy and not necessarily 'appreciated' in finer circles. He knew in the absence of such disclosures on his part that Dulci had her own theories about his actions, none of which showed him in a favourable light.

'You're not going to set up any kind of scheme, are you, such as the time you fleeced Wembley out of his thoroughbred over a game of Commerce?' She gave him a stern look and Jack could not hold back his laughter.

'What a little hypocrite you are, m'dear. Why should you have all the fun? Besides, Wembley deserved it.' Jack leaned close to her ear, inhaling the light scent of lavender, fresh and beguiling like the temptress who wore it. 'I heard you won a racing dare in Richmond last week.'

Dulci looked momentarily alarmed. 'No one is supposed to know. Who told you?' She stopped herself in mid-question and shook her head. 'Never mind, there were only two of us who knew. I know very well who told you.' She made a pretty pout. 'I thought Lord Amberston would know better.'

Jack laughed. 'Don't worry, your reputation is intact. However, it does occur to me that you play awfully close to the fire—does society know their darling Incomparable dabbles in scandal on a regular basis?'

Dulci would not be diverted. 'This is not about me, Jack. I want your word. I don't want you playing cards with Señor Ortiz.'

Jack was all mock solemnity. 'I promise you, this is not about cards.' Such a suggestion was almost laughable if the situation wasn't so serious. She could no more conceive of stopping a war before it started than he could conceive of having nothing more serious to worry about than a card game. The damnable thing was, he could not tell her otherwise.

'Do you promise?' Dulci was sceptical of his easy acquiescence.

'You have my word, Dulci. In exchange, I want yours that there will be no more moonlight horse racing in Richmond. That's dangerous. You should know better than to risk your neck and your horse's.'

'Now who's the hypocrite?' Dulci flashed a teasing smile that showed off the dimple in her cheek. 'You're hardly the arbiter of moral fashion. I remember a few years ago when you masqueraded as a fop to help Brandon catch the Cat of Manchester. That escapade ran fairly close to outright law breaking. My horse race was merely ill advised.'

Jack managed a smile at the memory. 'That's the

best service I've ever rendered your brother. I got him a wife in the bargain and he's been happy ever since.'

Dulci held his gaze, returning his smile. Something warm flickered to life in those blue eyes of hers. Jack moved her close to him as they turned. She did not resist his subtle possession. Jack gave her a private, knowing look. He knew she was remembering the thrill of their exploits to save Nora, the midnight wedding ceremony where Brandon, the earl, had married the notorious Cat. Perhaps she was remembering the dangerous sparks of desire that had risen suddenly and unbidden in the orangery at Christmas.

'Don't, Jack,' Dulci cautioned him softly.

'Don't what, Dulci?' Jack prodded with a whisper, knowing full well her thoughts had gone in the same direction as his, his body enjoying the feel of her far more than it should on a ballroom floor. 'Don't remember you in the orangery? Your hair coming down, your lips wet and red, your face tilted up in the candlelight waiting for my kiss? Your body pressed to mine as close as two bodies can be with their clothes on? How can I forget when I've seen you like that in my mind every night since?' The moment had been unpredictably heady. For a man with his vast experience with women, his reaction had played havoc with his senses whenever he recalled it, which was far too often for his own good.

Nothing had proved its equal, although Jack had certainly tried in the ensuing months. Dulci was a woman who demanded all of a man and that was far too dangerous of a commitment for him to make, for her as well as himself. But he was flirting shamelessly now, seducing her with words, his body and mind firing at the thrill of the challenge she presented.

He saw the pulse in her neck race at his words, belying the protest on her lips. 'Don't remember, Jack. We both know it was a mistake and it will be a mistake again.'

'I don't make mistakes when it comes to seduction, Dulci.'

'No, but afterwards you make plenty. Your *seductus exitus* needs work.'

'That's not a real Latin phrase.'

'*Exitus* is and it doesn't change the fact that yours needs work.'

'Only practice makes perfect.' Jack gave a heavy sigh of over-exaggerated disappointment. 'Alas, I have so few chances to practise.'

'That's not what I hear.'

Jack had no desire to talk about those particular rumours—rumours that involved a certain actress, strawberries and a large grain of the truth. If he could get Dulci away from the crowds, away from the eyes that watched their every move, maybe they could just talk, maybe something more. He *did* want to talk. He wanted to find out what she knew about the Venezuelans. Then again, who was he fooling? He wanted to do more than talk. He wanted to see if the sensations were still there. Perhaps Christmas had been an anomaly. It was a risky proposition at best, especially if he was wrong, but tonight his better judgement was no match for Dulci in pomegranate silk and memories of hot kisses.

'A walk in the garden then, Dulci,' Jack breathed against her ear, inhaling the lavender rinse of her hair. He could feel her body giving in, no matter what arguments her mind made. He could feel it answering to his, fickle compatriots to the codes of decency and honour that demanded they take a different route.

'All right, but just a walk,' Dulci consented.

Jack murmured low at her ear, 'I'm sure there'll be something handy to throw at me if you need it.' His hand tightened at her waist, ushering her towards the French doors that led outside. Ballrooms might be for business, but gardens…well, gardens were for pleasure.

The garden with Jack was a bad idea. *Anything* with Jack was a bad idea as she very well knew from gossip and brief personal experience. He had a reputation for a reason, actually several reasons. Dulci wasn't regretting her consent to walk in the garden, but she was *going* to. She knew it and yet she allowed him to lead her down both the proverbial and literal garden path, because she'd been able to think of nothing else since Christmas and Jack was irresistible, flaws and all.

There were definitely plenty of flaws, which worked only to heighten her own curiosity regarding the man behind the rumours—where did he go when he disappeared from London for months on end? What service had he rendered King William that had catapulted a poor squire's son into the ranks of the peerage with a hereditary title? How true was the tittle-tattle circulating behind ladies' fans that Jack was a lover beyond compare? There was probably a reason curiosity killed the cat, Dulci thought. She'd do better to forget such sordid things and to hope that Jack didn't read minds.

It was proving more difficult than expected to banish such thoughts at the moment. Jack drew her aside, slightly off the garden path, having arrived at his intended destination, a small alcove with a burbling fountain and a stone bench, the moon overhead and the paper lanterns that festively lined the garden paths giving off enough light to wander without fear of tripping.

It was a setting that showed Jack to great advantage. The moonlight cast a silvery hue to his winter-wheat hair, giving it the appearance of a smooth, sleek mane, every hair in place. The subtle detail work of his tailor emphasised the breadth of his shoulders, the trimness of his waist and the length of his legs, a reminder that while turned out in the guise of an immaculate, well-groomed gentleman, there was a raw, rough power beneath the clothes, signs of a man who'd led a life full of varied experiences.

Dulci often wondered if anyone else saw that quality in Jack. The longer she knew him, the more she didn't know him. He was a master of illusion. One only saw what Jack wanted to show and she'd been as easily duped on occasion as the rest.

She no more knew what truly drove Jack than any other member of the *ton*. She'd like to know more. Since the night in the orangery she'd been thinking rather a lot about Jack, her attentions drawn to whatever rumour was circulating about him any given week. She'd heard since Christmas he'd been busy kissing Lady Scofield in her big gardens at Lambeth.

A delicious tremor shot through Dulci. Had he truly brought her out here, into this garden, to do the same? Would she, *should* she, let him? Those Christmas kisses had dominated too much of her mind. She couldn't deny the truth; she wanted Jack to kiss her and perhaps do more than kiss her. Her body could not forget the heat Jack's hands had invoked, the need for something more that his body had awakened in hers. She wanted to feel that way again, wanted him to wake her again.

She opted for a show of sophistication. She didn't want Jack thinking she was overly eager if he actually had seduction on his mind. Nor did she want to be over-eager if he *didn't*; such a miscalculation would be embarrassing and only serve to stoke his already over-inflated sense of self-importance.

'What now, Jack?' Dulci gave him a practised, coy smile. She moved into the alcove, surveying its furnishings with an assessing look. 'The fountain is probably not an option, but perhaps the bench is a possibility.'

'Did you consider I might not have asked you out here to seduce you? I seem to recall in the ballroom that you were rankly against such a venue.' Jack leaned against a stone column at the alcove's entrance, looking urbane and relaxed, very much at home with the situation. But Dulci could feel his eyes, hot and direct, following her movements. She could not fool him for long. He was experienced enough to know the game was afoot.

'Since when has that ever stopped you, Jack? The

greater the challenge, the harder you try.' She trailed a hand in the fountain.

'I have been known to rise to the occasion.' Jack grinned wickedly and stepped towards her. 'I have the firmest of resolves, or so I've been told.'

She recognised that *cicisbeo* smile of his all too well. It was his stock in trade in London ballrooms, the smile that said she was the centre of his attention, that every wish, every desire was about to be fulfilled and more. She'd seen many women believe it. It was easy to believe that smile. She believed in it now against better sense.

Dulci stepped backwards, striving to create more space between them. She had not come to the Fotheringay ball looking for this. Indeed, she had not expected to find Jack here at all. The Season was too young. She'd thought she'd have a few weeks to herself before Jack came to wreak havoc on her senses. She'd thought she'd heard he was out of town. 'You've gathered all the other women to your banner tonight, Jack. You have no need of me as well.'

'But you're the only one I want.' Jack was grinning broadly now. Drat him, he knew he had her on the run.

'No, it's simply your arrogance, Jack. You can't stand not having every woman in the room swooning at your feet.'

Jack laughed, the sharp planes of his aristocratic face melting into boyish playfulness. 'By Jove, Dulci, no one quite cuts me down to size like you do, and goodness knows on occasion I need it.' He looked ten years younger, whatever secret cares he bore dissolving, minimising the darkness and mystery that limned him like a nimbus around the sun since his return to England. It occurred to her to wonder what he'd been like before? Surely he hadn't always been this way? How did a man become like Jack?

'Dulci.' The sound of her name on his lips was an invitation to sin. It was enough and it succeeded where all Jack's calculated foreplay had fallen short. She was in his arms in an instant, letting her body savour the strength of him, the feel of him, the almond scent of his soap, letting her mind forget all the reasons this was going to be a bad idea. His mouth took hers in a long, slow kiss, teasing her with its languorous exploration, one hand at the back of her neck, fingers entwined in her hair. The heat in her started to rise.

'I'm sorry about the orangery, Dulci,' Jack murmured, with sincere penitence. How could she not forgive him? Then something caught her eye over Jack's shoulder and she froze, her mind remembering all the reasons.

Jack nuzzled her neck encouragingly. 'Dulci, this is where you say you're sorry too about throwing that pot and you run your hands through my hair looking for any remnants of that damnable lump you gave me.'

'I don't think so, Jack.' Dulci pushed against his chest and stepped back, the moment lost to reality and disappointment. She'd been so ready to believe. She gave a flick of her head, nodding for Jack to turn around. It was the orangery all over again.

A throat cleared in the nominal darkness. A nervous, blushing page dressed in the royal livery of Hanover stammered his message. 'Excuse me, my lord. I have an urgent message from Clarence House. I was told to find you and tell you to come at once.'

Dulci watched Jack straighten his shoulders almost imperceptibly, the boyish pleasure that had so recently wreathed his face instantly subdued. The transformation happened so swiftly, it was possible to think she'd imagined the other. Jack pressed a few coins into the messenger's hand, no doubt meant to buy his silence regarding where and how the boy had found the viscount and sent him on before turning back to her.

'Dulci, I'm sorry. I have to leave. May I escort you back inside?' He was all duty now. Did this happen with all his women or was it just her bad luck? She hadn't heard, but then again she couldn't imagine anyone wanting to brag Jack had thrown them over for a government summons.

'What could the king want this time of night? Isn't he off to his own clubs and entertainments?' Dulci had recognised the address immediately: the residence of William IV.

'England never sleeps, Dulci.' Jack gave her a kind smile that she found condescending.

'Don't patronise me, Jack,' Dulci snapped.

'I'll call on you tomorrow,' Jack offered. But she would have none of his olive-branch brand of pity.

'I will not be home to you. I am not going to become one of your easy women who let you kiss them whenever you pass through town.' Dulci pushed past him, angrier at herself than at him. Jack would always be Jack, whoever that really was. As much time as she'd spent listening to rumours she'd thought she'd have understood that by now. She would find her own way back inside and, after a decent interval, she'd leave. The night had lost its lustre. But he halted her with a warm chuckle that said he didn't believe her bluff for a moment.

'You can't ignore me, Dulci. Very well, don't receive me. But I will see you tomorrow night. At the Danby rout, if you remember,' Jack called softly. 'I'll be the one in azure. Perhaps we can rename the ball the Blue Danby ball. It can be our private joke.'

She didn't want anything 'private' with Jack. Dulci fisted her hands in her gown where no one could see, her temper rising. It was just like Jack to make a joke when she was mad. Damn it all. She'd already forgot about the wager. She allowed herself the unladylike luxury of stomping her foot in frustration on the garden path. She'd known from the start coming out here with Jack was a bad idea; anything with Jack was a bad idea as she'd proven yet again. At least she'd have plenty to berate herself with on the lonely carriage ride home.

The carriage was crowded for all that there was only one person in it, thanks to the enormity of her thoughts, Dulci groused an hour later. She felt slightly better thinking it was Jack's fault, but that wasn't entirely true. He'd merely opened Pandora's box with his kisses and let loose all nature of strange feelings and emotions into her world. Hopefully common sense hadn't got out with the rest. Maybe it still hung there like a butterfly with one wing caught in the closed box lid, the other wing struggling for release. It certainly wasn't still in the box—tonight had illustrated that. At best, she had only half of it left.

Jack had awakened the curiosities of both mind and body. She was twenty-six and seriously doubted she would ever make a marriage that suited her temperament. But that didn't stop her from wanting to know the mysteries of the marriage bed, the secrets of satisfying the passions of the body.

She was not so naïve as to be unaware that a certain calibre of gentleman had offered to solve that mystery for her. To date, she'd always been quick to scotch any efforts in the direction. Some risks were simply not worth taking. The kind of gentleman who offered such gratification was not the kind of gentleman who would keep her secrets. Good heavens, Amberston hadn't even kept their horse race secret. One could only guess what someone like him would do with an even bigger secret.

Jack was different. The shocking thought nearly jolted her off the carriage seat. An idea came to Dulci. Why not Jack? Any woman with eight seasons behind her, virgin or not, knew when a man desired her and Jack had wanted her. Perhaps he only wanted her for a night, for the novelty of it.

Whatever his motives, he did want her and that was all that mattered. If his wanting lasted only a night, so much the better. She was looking to satisfy her curiosity, nothing long term. Jack had already proven he could wake her passions and he'd already proven he could be discreet. He kept secrets for the Empire. He could surely keep one short liaison from public consumption and he would never tell Brandon.

Dulci tapped her chin with a gloved finger. Hmm. Brandon might be a sticking point. She would have to overcome any resistance his friendship with Brandon might pose. Then she laughed out loud in the empty carriage at the ridiculous notions passing through her head. She was actually sitting here planning how to seduce the notorious Viscount Wainsbridge! She needed her head examined. What woman of virtue deliberately gave away her greatest asset? Moreover, in her numerous seasons she'd seen with her own eyes what happened to the young girls who'd fallen prey to various pre-marital temptations. The world wasn't big enough for a fallen woman.

A wicked voice whispered its rebuttal: *only if you get caught. You haven't been caught yet. Jack's perfect— discreet, skilled and in no mood to get caught himself. He might even empathise with you...*

She could laugh all night at the odd ideas floating through her mind, but Dulci could not quell the growing sense that in spite of all the decent reasons not to go through with it, she just might.

Chapter Three

Jack Hanley, the *first* Viscount Wainsbridge for all of five years, always answered the king's summons to Clarence House with alacrity and anxiety no matter what time of day or night it came or whose bed it found him in. Alacrity because one did not keep his monarch waiting, especially when one possessed a title as new as his. Anxiety because he knew the summons was merely a prelude to upheaval. William would not have called him if something had not been afoot that needed his special attentions. No doubt there'd been a development with the Venezuelans, but he was suspicious that it had occurred so quickly. He'd only met them an hour ago.

'I need you to stop a war.' William said abruptly as Jack entered. Jack merely nodded as if such statements were commonplace conversation and shut the door of the Clarence House study behind him. He had suspected as much. The initial rumours had been confirmed, then.

'When, your Majesty?' He took in the room with a

sweeping glance, nodding curtly to the third man present, Viscount Gladstone from the Foreign Office.

William IV toyed idly with a paperweight. 'The war hasn't precisely happened yet. But I have it on good authority from Gladstone here that it will if we don't take steps now.'

Ah, it was to be a pre-emptive action then. He was good at that. Jack took the liberty of pouring himself a brandy at the sideboard. He took a seat and expertly flipped up the tails of his evening wear, sliding a careful glance at Gladstone. He had personal reasons for not liking the man. Gladstone made no secret of his contempt for Jack's inferior birth and first-generation title. But professionally, the man possessed an astonishing acumen for foreign intelligence.

'Tell Wainsbridge what you've told me,' William said.

Gladstone cleared his throat. 'Venezuela is contesting its shared borders with British Guiana. They wish to extend their boundaries. It goes without saying that we are not interested in giving up our claims to that territory.' Gladstone stood up and walked to a long table, gesturing for Jack to follow.

With a long finger, Gladstone traced the boundaries on a map spread before them. 'The border in question is south-east of the Essequibo River.'

Jack nodded. He was one of the few who understood the magnitude of rivers in British Guiana. The marshy topography of British Guiana made coastal rivers the only thoroughfares into the interior. 'This is no small contention. We're dealing with approximately thirty-thousand square miles of property.' In a land of marshes and rivers, such territory was worth squabbling over.

Jack looked up from the map, back to where William sat. This information was not new to him. Indeed, it had been at the root of his presence at the Fotheringay ball. What he didn't know were the motives behind it. 'Do we have any speculations as to why Venezuela is suddenly interested in this section of territory?'

For centuries, ever since Britain had first staked a claim to Guiana in the sixteen hundreds, Spain had not done more than establish a handful of missions along the border. The border had been undefined and peaceful. Of course, it was an independent Venezuela now, not Spain that shared the border. Perhaps after a little over ten years of independence, Venezuela was flexing its muscle in the region.

'That's where you come in, Wainsbridge.' William leaned back in his chair, hands steepled.

'Of course, anything, your Majesty. I am always at your service,' Jack said easily, hiding his apprehension. He'd had to train himself over the last few years to stay alert in William's presence. The man acted more like a retired naval officer—which he was—than royalty— which had been a far-fetched possibility once. It was easy to forget that the tall, white-haired man with a soft chin and friendly eyes commanded a nation. Being with the man felt almost ordinary, like being with a beloved uncle until one remembered that, unlike the uncle who could be refused, one could not refuse the king.

'As you know, you've been asked to determine how

real rumours of this border dispute are. I am interested in hearing how your evening went with the Venezuelan delegation.'

'I met them, but just barely.' Jack eyed Gladstone suspiciously. None of this was urgent or beyond what he already knew. Why the emergency summons?

Gladstone flicked a glance at William. 'There's been a further development. One of the gentlemen in the delegation is heavily influenced by a private and powerful consortium of Venezuelan businessmen who are eager to profit from the boundary dispute. We want to identify him as quickly as possible. It is believed the gentleman, whoever he is, may be in possession of a forged map that shows Venezuela's "preferred" boundaries. He may try to pass it off as a legitimate document and use it as evidence to force a new treaty of limits.'

Jack immediately thought of Calisto Ortiz, his smooth manners and his 'ombudsman' attachment to the delegation—official but unofficial. Jack returned to his chair and sat back to give his report.

'I think we can eliminate Adalberto Vargas. He's the senior member, in his early fifties. From his manners tonight, he's from a more traditional school of diplomacy. He's not likely to be swayed by such risky and underhanded tactics like a forged map.

'Neither would it be Hector Dias. He does not have either the suave mannerisms of Ortiz or the intellectual background of Vargas.' Jack surmised Hector Dias was a man who'd no doubt begun his career in mid-level staff positions with various embassies and would likely end his career there as well. The cut and cloth of his clothes at the ball had certainly suggested as much. The man hadn't the wealth at his disposal to match the wardrobes of Ortiz or Vargas.

'So that leaves Calisto Ortiz,' Gladstone put in, a note of triumph in his voice that it had been so easy to detect a likely candidate.

'Yes. He's the flamboyant charmer of the group. He's also there as an ombudsman, so the rules he must follow are much more lax than the other two. His English is excellent, and his connections even more so. He's a nephew to one of the regional Venezuelan viceroys with family connections to the governor. He's a likely choice.'

'We'll start putting together a more detailed dossier on him now that we know what to look for,' Gladstone said. 'If he's so well connected, British intelligence surely has information on his family. Perhaps he's organising a plantation movement. Plantations are big business in that part of the world.'

'Not *that* big,' Jack scoffed at the theory. Gladstone scowled at him, the old antagonism between them rising.

'I'd love to hear your ideas,' Gladstone retorted.

Choosing to ignore the slight, Jack returned to the map and stared thoughtfully at the outlined area, an idea forming in his mind. Businessmen weren't interested in the natural beauty of a land. There was something lucrative in the river valley, a valuable resource.

He spoke a single word to the room at large. 'Gold.'

'Gold?' Gladstone replied, incredulous.

'You forget, I've actually been to the region. I was

there in 1830 after I helped Schomburgk on his Anegada expedition.' Jack smoothly interjected his credentials into the conversation. His work there had laid the grounds for being awarded the viscountcy. 'The river valleys are too wet and the forests in the interior are too dense for serious farming. Businessmen aren't looking to put up a plantation community in this region. No profit.' Gladstone looked like he'd gladly throttle him.

William broke in to defuse the tension. 'We want to be certain in regards to what they're after. We can use that knowledge to grease negotiations if we must. Until then, Wainsbridge, Ortiz is yours. I want to know what has made the area an urgent point of interest and how far they're willing to go to get it.'

Dismissed, they took their leave of the monarch and made their way through Clarence House to the front door. Jack was glad he had his coach. He did not want to share a hackney with Gladstone. They stepped out into the night air.

Jack's coach waited at the kerb but Gladstone couldn't resist a final jab as Jack stepped up to the door. 'I hear we have a mutual acquaintance in Lady Dulcinea Wycroft.'

'You hear the most amazing things, Gladstone,' Jack returned.

'I see them too, sometimes,' came Gladstone's cryptic reply.

'You've never got over Lady Dulcinea jilting you.' Jack's reply was cool, but inside he was seething. Gladstone must have had men watching the ballroom that night, checking out the Venezuelan delegation on his own even though Jack had been given the job. He would not put it past Gladstone to have forced a meeting tonight simply to drag him away from Dulci.

Anger clouded Gladstone's face. 'Behind those clothes you're nothing but a scrapper, a no-account country squire's son. I can only imagine how many boots you had to lick to rise this far.'

'Whereas I am sure you're quite clear on the boots you've had to lick. No imagining there. Your family's been currying favour since the sixteen hundreds. Dirty business that, two centuries of boot-licking.' Jack stepped into his coach and held the door open for a moment. 'Goodnight, Gladstone.'

He slammed the coach door and sank back against the squabs, less sanguine than he'd let on. This was dicey business with the Venezuelan delegation. Negotiations of this nature were always very covert, hardly ever making the public news, but that didn't make them less dangerous. Usually, they were more so. Without the check and balance of being in the public eye, there were no rules to govern them. Still, it would be business as usual if Dulci wasn't involved. But she was—placed right at the centre of the storm because of her connection to the three men most intrinsically concerned. There was going to be trouble. He could feel it in his bones.

Dulci Wycroft firmly believed trouble found you when you least expected it. She had an antidote for that: she expected trouble.

Always.

She'd learned early that collecting artefacts wasn't exactly an old maid's safe hobby. Not that she thought of herself as an old maid, although she'd reached the august age of twenty-six, trailing a string of six refusals of marriage behind her. Nor was she looking for safe.

If she was, she wouldn't be here, or a lot of the other places she'd been. Her hand flexed and closed around the small gun in her pocket, her sharp eyes alert to any suspicious movements in the dim interior of the dockside warehouse. Warehouses in the dock districts were not foreign venues to her. But this one, set in a rough part of Southwark, was by far the worst.

She'd been glad she'd decided to bring her own unmarked coach instead of relying on public hansom cabs. She'd noticed that the deeper into the area she'd journeyed the presence of cabs had dried up, a sure testimony to the unsavoury nature of the environs, the noise and comparable respectability of Hays Wharf far behind them.

A man moved from the shadows. Dulci tensed and then relaxed. She might not completely trust this man, but she knew him. He was her reason for being here in these rather questionable surroundings.

He strode forwards, well-dressed and olive skinned. *'Señorita, buenos días!'* he effused, lavishly bowing over her hand, too lavishly. Sweat lightly beaded his upper lip and Dulci noted immediately that the lavish gesture was a mask for the man's anxiety. The usual self-confidence the man possessed seemed oddly absent today.

Dulci withdrew her hand as soon as it was politely

possible, her tones haughty and clipped. 'Señor Vasquez, let us dispense with the pleasantries. What do you have for me that is so urgent it could not wait out the afternoon?' Señor Vasquez's note had ruled out the chance to catch the Royal Geographic Society's lecture on the West Indies in its entirety, but with luck she might still make the last part.

'I have artefacts from the Americas.' He gestured towards an opened crate, but Dulci didn't miss the quick dart of his eyes.

'Are you expecting anyone else, *señor*?' Dulci asked keenly, her own eyes conducting a quick investigation of the warehouse too.

'I have many appointments, *señorita*. I merely wish you to see these items privately. They're from Venezuela, your latest area of interest.'

'Really?' Dulci replied coolly, raising her eyebrows a fraction of an inch to indicate only mild appreciation. A display of unabashed delight would only serve to increase Señor Vasquez's price.

Dulci reached into the crate with one hand, parting the straw packing with one gloved hand. The other hand cautiously remained in her pocket, her eyes unwaveringly fixed on Señor Vasquez. Her hand met with stone and she pulled out a carved statue. Vasquez did indeed know her interests well.

'It's a *zemi*.' Dulci fought hard to keep the rising excitement out of her voice, studying the object reverently in the poor light. The idol was devoid of any garments and the stone carving indicated breasts and a rounded belly. 'It's an idol of a native god, or goddess in this case. Unless I am completely mistaken, this is a fertility fetish.' She stared at him in stark contemplation, oblivious to his discomfort at such frank discussion. 'Did this come with a—?'

'A bowl?' Vasquez finished for her. 'But of course, *señorita*.' His eyes flashed with a mocking chagrin. 'I would not give you only part of a set.'

Dulci set down the carving and with both hands delved beneath the straw packing. She felt the shallow dip of a bowl. 'Yes, there it is.' She withdrew a stone bowl and set it in place. 'There, Señor Vasquez, you can see how it all goes together. The idols are flat headed so that a stone bowl can be placed on top of their heads for worship.'

'*Buena, señorita.* Name a price, and it shall be yours.'

He seemed far too eager to get rid of her after the demanding note requiring an immediate meeting.

'I would prefer to see the rest of the contents,' Dulci said, proceeding to empty the crate and offering an exposition on each piece she extracted. 'This is likely to be an amulet, this would be a *metate*, they used it for grinding seeds…' She spoke absently, more to herself than for the edification of Señor Vasquez.

Dulci dusted off her hands and surveyed the artefacts, seven in all. She was cognisant of the fact that Señor Vasquez had checked his watch twice while she'd unloaded the crate. He was clearly expecting someone else, or perhaps hoping to avoid the expected visitor. The collection was certainly splendid, but, while it was exciting to her, she had not forgot the urgency of Vasquez's summons. 'Is this everything?'

'All but this final item.' Vasquez handed her a worn leather book the size of a journal.

She eyed him speculatively. 'Saving the best for last?'

Vasquez placed a hand over his heart. 'I seek only to please you, *señorita*. I know much you like to read. Look here, there's even a few maps, very detailed.'

Dulci thumbed the pages, noting the drawings of strange plants and places. 'An explorer's journal? Perhaps a missionary's log?' Dulci asked. It was written in English and she immediately thought of Jack. The journal would make a fine gift for him, a remembrance of his own work in that region a few years back. Not that he deserved such a gift after last night, she reminded herself.

'I can only guess, *señorita*. My English is not good enough for reading,' Vasquez hedged. 'I am a mere importer.'

Dulci was instantly suspicious. There was nothing 'mere' about Vasquez. The Spaniard was rich, his wealth made from the lucre of Spanish interests in South America. 'How did you come by this book?'

Vasquez shrugged gallantly. 'It was in the same crate as the statue. It was on the last ship. I unpacked it and thought of you, that is all.'

Nothing was ever that straightforward. When it was, it was time to start asking the hard questions. 'Are the artefacts stolen?' Dulci cocked her head to one side in an assessing tilt. She'd done business with Vasquez before. He'd proven to be a reliable contact, visiting

London twice a year from Spain. Still, something didn't seem quite right.

'Of course not, I am a legitimate importer. Such chicanery would damage my reputation,' Vasquez argued, putting on an offended air at the suggestion.

'If they're not stolen, then why the urgency? We had an appointment tomorrow morning. What difference can a day make?'

'Ah, yes, *señorita*, please forgive me for worrying you. I must leave for home on the morning tide instead of leaving later in the week as I had planned. It is a personal matter. I did not want to leave without meeting with you.' He lowered his voice conspiratorially. 'There are others who were interested in the artefacts. I am to meet with them tonight. But I confess I wanted you to have first pick.'

Dulci nodded, her concern ebbing slightly in the wake of his explanation. The man was a consummate salesman. No doubt he'd arranged all this to increase his price. Urgency was a well-proven ploy for adding spice to a negotiation. 'I'll pay one hundred pounds for the crate and the journal.'

'One hundred pounds? *Madre de dios*, but I could not part with them for such a sum.' He protested neatly. 'Surely you understand, *señorita*, the effort to transport such goods across the Atlantic and bring them to London?'

Dulci's tone was brisk. 'Surely *you* understand, I am in no mood to haggle like a fishwife in the market. I am late for a much-anticipated lecture and you are fully cognisant of the fairness of my price.'

'Because you are my favourite, I will indulge you.' Vasquez relented with an exaggerated shrug. 'A hundred pounds, *señorita*.'

Dulci gave a curt nod. 'Deliver the crate to my town house promptly and you'll receive instructions for payment. If you are quick, you'll have no trouble getting your money before you sail. As always, *señor*, it is a pleasure.'

Vasquez bent over her hand. 'The pleasure is most assuredly mine.'

The pretty *señorita* had barely exited the building before he began rapidly packing up the artefacts. The sooner this crate was out of his hands, the better. He had not told her any lies: the artefacts were not stolen and he did have an urgent personal need to sail tomorrow— he valued his health. Having those artefacts found in his possession would endanger that health greatly.

It had recently come to his notice through his vast networks that someone highly placed in the Venezuelan government wanted them in deadly earnest. The artefacts didn't look particularly dangerous or valuable, just stone and wood carvings, most of them done with a crude skill at best.

It didn't matter. They could have been jewel studded and he'd still have wanted to be rid of them. Originally, he'd thought to make a tidy profit on them, but whoever wanted them had not wanted to purchase them. There'd been no interest in a business transaction. Whatever the reason, these items had not been meant to be seen by others. The possessor of these artefacts, for reasons he could not ascertain, was as good as dead. The artefacts were out of his hands now. He was safe. He'd been careful to erase any mention of them in his ship's manifesto and if his London warehouse was searched, they would find nothing that traced the artefacts back to him.

He didn't worry overmuch about the artefacts being discovered in the eccentric Señorita Wycroft's possession. If the artefacts couldn't be traced to him, they couldn't be traced to her. He supposed it was entirely possible the objects could be found through other avenues, but that would be a random happenstance completely out of his control. In all probability, the artefacts and whatever they hid would fall into obscurity, displayed inside a nice glass curio case in the *señorita*'s town house. His ethical conscience, such as it was, was clear. Señor Vasquez closed the lid on the crate and breathed a much-desired sigh of relief.

Chapter Four

Calisto Ortiz aimed a frustrated kick at an empty packing crate and swore in a fluid torrent of Spanish for all to hear. There was inept and then there was outright incompetence. His men had bungled the job again. How hard was it to retrieve a map no one knew existed? Yet his men had failed to recover it in Venezuela after the map-maker had mistakenly packed it with his other archaeological finds for shipping back to Spain. Here in London, the map had slipped from their grasp a second time. After having tracked it to an importer named Vasquez, Ortiz had thought his work was nearly done. He simply had to run Vasquez to ground and claim the map. But he was too late. The warehouse was deserted, but only freshly so. The crates were empty and bore the markings of Spanish freight. They also looked new, lacking the dirt and gouges that often accompanied crates over time.

Calisto Ortiz barked out new orders to his men.

'Search the docks, maybe the ship hasn't sailed yet. Search the taverns and inns for Vasquez too.'

The men rushed to do his bidding, leaving him alone in the warehouse. Calisto upended a crate and sat down upon it, heaving a sigh. He cared less about finding the ship than he did about finding Vasquez. Vasquez was fast becoming a valuable link in this game for two reasons. The first reason was of a practical nature. If he didn't find Vasquez and hence the map, it would mean the map was loose in London. The search would take on a needle-in-the-haystack quality.

The second reason was more symbolic. Vasquez was moving fast. By all reports the ship had only been in London a short time ahead of his own arrival and now it was potentially gone, the warehouse cleared out. Vasquez knew he had something dangerous and he'd come to London to pass it on to someone, to unburden himself. It meant the map was no longer a well-guarded secret. The mission had now taken on two goals: retrieve the map *and* silence those who knew about it.

Ortiz ran his hands through his dark hair, breathing deeply to calm his racing mind. He had to take one step at a time, one assumption at a time. Until he found Vasquez, he had no way of knowing if Vasquez understood the value of the map. It could be that Vasquez only knew he had something of dubious worth, but didn't know what it was. Along with the map, there were figurines, *zemis* and *metates*. Then of course, he'd have to hunt down whomever Vasquez had sold the items to.

He had to be prepared for best- and worst-case

scenarios, the best being that the map had passed from hand to hand without anyone detecting its importance. The worst was that Vasquez did know the significance of the map and had sold it for a nice profit to someone who'd appreciate the map's value in the discussions that would soon open up between the Venezuelan delegation and the British government in regards to the questionable border Venezuela shared with British Guiana.

Calisto knew he played a dangerous double game, not only with the British but with the Venezuelan government as well—not that the latter would mind if they came out the victor. Some would claim the map was a forgery, but Calisto preferred to think of the map merely as potentially biased. He wouldn't be the first person in history to sponsor a map-maker to tweak the boundaries a bit here and there. In all reality, the interior of British Guiana was so underexplored, who could say where the borders really were?

It would take years to disprove the boundaries on his map and ownership was nine-tenths of the law, as the saying went. In the meanwhile, Venezuela would be in possession of a very lucrative piece of land containing riches untold and he and his uncle would be wealthy men.

Everything would work out. He was a man who knew how to cover his tracks and follow all necessary leads. His men were hunting down Vasquez right now. There was nothing more he could do at the moment. He flipped open his pocket watch. He had just enough time to change and dine before the Danby rout. With luck, the delectable Lady Dulcinea would be in attendance without her surly polyglot friend.

Luck was in short supply all around. The Danby rout was fully engaged by the time Jack arrived. He'd meant to come earlier in hopes of stealing a moment with Dulci before she was surrounded. He'd wanted to set the record straight about their most unfortunate interruption the prior evening. It was not how he imagined their reunion. But business had conspired against him. He'd spent the afternoon discreetly following Calisto Ortiz to an empty warehouse in a seedy part of Southwark.

The unplanned adventure had been enlightening, posing several interesting questions, such as why a man of Ortiz's station would be down at the docks. Ortiz's behaviour had been telling as well. There was no doubt that whatever had taken place in the warehouse upset Ortiz greatly. As to what that might have been, Jack could only speculate. Although he'd explored the warehouse after Ortiz's departure, he'd found nothing more than the same empty, Spanish-stamped crates that had upset Ortiz. By the time he'd reported his news to Gladstone and picked up his newly tailored waistcoat of deep periwinkle blue, afternoon had swiftly turned into evening, leaving him hard pressed to find time for a much-needed bath and *toilette* before setting out for the night.

There was no hope of catching Dulci alone, a fact attested to by the sea of blue surrounding her four men deep. Squaring his shoulders and setting aside the cares of the day, Jack cut through the crowd of admirers to place himself in front of her. He made a courtly leg. 'It appears I've more than fulfilled my commission, Lady Dulcinea.' Jack gestured to the various hues of blue assembled about her. 'I do believe I've saved the economy for a day.'

Dulci laughed and waved her fan, a painted affair that matched the pale blue hues of her gown. 'Tailors' apprentices across the city are in your debt, Wainsbridge.'

'Certainly that's worth a dance.' Jack offered a charming grin and held out his hand.

There was the sound of grumbling. A few voices were raised in complaint: 'He's stealing all the best dances.' 'He danced with her last night.'

Dulci squashed the protests with a smile. Between her gown and that smile, she looked like an angel come to earth as she moved to take his hand. Her beauty never ceased to entrance him. But Jack knew better than to be misled. If Dulci Wycroft was any kind of angel, she was an avenging one. Before he could make his peace with her, she was going to make him pay. Would she start with the wager or the interruption from last night?

'This deep periwinkle is an improvement, Jack.' Ah, it was to be the wager. 'Still, it's a far cry from what you used to wear. I remember in Manchester you had an evening coat with diamond buttons. Brandon said you wore it to his betrothal ball. Whatever happened to all those shirts with yards of lace for cuffs?'

'I burnt them,' Jack answered succinctly. 'I have not played the fop for years now. Such a façade does not suit a king's adviser.'

'It did once. You used to say people were unguarded in their conversation because they assumed a fop had stuffing for brains.' There she went, probing again for the things he could not tell her.

'I'm an adviser, not a spy. A man with stuff for brains is not a man who is ultimately respected. Playing the fop had rather obvious limitations after a while for an adviser.' Jack kept his answers abrupt.

'How long do you suppose we have before we'll be interrupted by a government summons tonight? Do you think we might make it through this dance?' Dulci quipped, with an edge to her voice that warned Jack he was not entirely forgiven.

Damn Gladstone and his interference. But Jack would not make excuses about who he was and what he did. He turned them sharply at the top of the ballroom and decided it was time to change the conversation to something lighter.

'I'm surprised you're angry over the interruption last night, Dulci. You were the one who didn't want to go out to the garden in the first place. Admit it, you like my kisses.' What was he doing? He was flirting with her as if he meant to take this interlude further. *Which of course you do*, his conscious prompted honestly. *Admit it, the experiment last night failed. The kisses at Christmas weren't an isolated incident. You burn for her.*

'They're pleasant enough when there's nothing better to do,' Dulci teased knowingly.

'Is there usually something better to do?' Jack challenged with a grin, liking the way her smile lit her face when she teased him, liking the confident, bold way she flirted. But he had to tread carefully here. Dulci could not be handled like the experienced married women of the *ton*. She was far finer than that and she'd expect far more than they if he led her down that path.

'There was today.'

'No more dangerous wagers in the moonlight, I hope.'

What he really hoped was that she hadn't spent any more time with Calisto Ortiz. He knew, of course, where Ortiz had been later in the afternoon, but that didn't preclude Ortiz having made an earlier call. From what Jack witnessed of the man on two occasions now, he wanted Ortiz as far from Dulci as possible.

'This morning I worked with my fencing instructor.'

Jack's eyebrows rose slightly at this. They rose further after the next pronouncement.

'Then, this afternoon, I picked up some new additions to my collection of artefacts from the new world. Your part of the world, actually. Somewhere near Venezuela, or maybe Guiana.'

'What collection is this?' An alarm rang somewhere deep inside him at her reference, but it would be premature to jump to conclusions.

Dulci's excitement was evident in the sparkle of her eyes as she explained. '*Zemis*, tribal fertility fetishes and other assorted items of interest. They're from the Arawak tribes.'

Alarm was no longer premature. The Arawaks lived on the south-eastern border near the Essequibo River. His well-trained face must have betrayed him momentarily because Dulci peered at him sharply.

'Have I shocked you?'

Very little shocked Jack after his travels. But that didn't mean he couldn't be terrified. His mind rushed to assimilate the information. This was far worse than his earlier concern over her involvement.

Last night he'd merely been concerned because she'd become a bystander who could be implicated, someone known to all three men: she was a woman in whom Ortiz was showing marked interest; she was the woman Gladstone had once aspired to marry; she was someone he'd paid recent social attentions to and that could put her at risk by association once Ortiz worked out his interest in the Venezuelan delegation. If Ortiz chose to strike out, Dulci would be a likely target.

But now her eccentric hobby had suddenly catapulted her into the forefront of the action. It begged the question whether Brandon had any idea what Dulci did with her time; first fencing and now this gadding about town collecting artefacts that were most likely stolen.

Was this merely coincidence or did Dulci actually possess the cargo Ortiz had been searching for? The dance was ending, but he could not return her to her court without knowing more. A strong urge to possess and protect her surged. He told himself the feeling was out of a sense of duty. With Brandon absent from town, it was his job to act as a surrogate protector. His more honest side didn't accept that lie for a moment. Something far deeper was at work here and it scared him.

'I had no idea your interests ran in that direction,' Jack said benignly, subtly ushering her towards the verandah.

'I have you to thank for my interest. After your work with Schomburgk, I turned my attentions from the Egyptian excavations to the New World. After all, these artefacts are from living tribes. They're clues to a way of life that is taking place right now, not thousands of years ago. I find that much more fascinating. I see you're surprised. There's a great deal you don't know about me, Jack.' Dulci laughed up at him, but not unkindly.

'Then tell me more,' Jack flirted, the coldness receding a bit. He was back in control now. He had a strategy. He would take her outside and quiz her thoroughly until he had his answers, kiss them out of her if need be. He'd probably kiss her anyway whether he needed to or not. 'Where did you come by these artefacts?'

'A Spanish importer named Vasquez has been supplying me with items over the past two years.'

A new type of alarm coursed through Jack, not all of it having to do with his concern over the current situation. Good lord, didn't the woman know the risks? Didn't she realise how easy it would be to buy stolen goods? The Americas were rife with men of questionable repute who looted tribal grave sites or stole religious icons from the natives in the hopes of selling them back home to unsuspecting purchasers.

Those were the honest men.

The dishonest men simply passed off imitations and forgeries as the real thing.

'I hope you're careful, Dulci,' Jack said. 'There are men who'd take advantage of a woman in that market.'

Dulci's reply was glib and self-assured. 'Oh, I am careful, I always take my gun.'

Jack gripped Dulci's arm, fear returning anew. 'Your *gun*? Where do you go?' He hadn't meant his comment in that way. He'd meant it as a warning about the quality of goods she was dealing with. But now, his concern grew exponentially. Clearly this Vasquez did not call safely at her home with his wares.

'To the wharves, of course, Jack.' Dulci fixed him with an incredulous look. 'Where else does one retrieve goods from ships?'

Oh God, oh God, this was getting worse by the moment. 'And today, Dulci? Did you go to the docks today? Where?'

Dulci's brow furrowed in puzzlement. She pulled her arm away. 'What is this, Jack? You didn't even know I collected until a few moments ago and now you're suddenly full of chivalrous concern for my well-being. I've been doing this far longer than you realise.'

It would do no good to worry Dulci. He'd be unable to tell her anything useful if she asked and that would only serve to anger her. Jack shrugged and dispatched a quick half-truth. 'There's been some concern about activity at the docks lately, that is all. It's been rougher than usual.'

'I went to Southwark and all was fine. Although I will admit that it was a section that was more run down than the usual areas I frequent. The artefacts are splendid. Their arrival is quite timely with the Venezuelan delegation in town. I am looking forward to showing them to Señor Ortiz. He may know something more about them than what I can find in the libraries. I want to write an article for the Royal Geographic Society about them.'

No! All of Jack's instincts rebelled at the notion of Dulci showing Ortiz. But he could not overtly steer her away from the man without raising suspicions or looking like a jealous suitor. Neither was an appealing prospect. Well, he'd just have to get there first.

'I'd like to see your collection. I can serve in Ortiz's place. Perhaps I'll recognise some of the items and be able to shed some further light on them. I have an inspiration—let's take a night off from all this social whirl. I'll call tomorrow evening after dinner. We can fence and I'll tell you if your instructor is any good. Afterwards, we can go over the collection.'

It was an audacious request. A gentleman never called on a lady at such a time and Jack was inviting himself. If it had been anyone else, his intentions would be clear. But Dulci was also a family friend. He was trading on that connection quite liberally with the request.

'Do you think you can best me, Jack?' Dulci's eyes twinkled with challenge at the mention of fencing. 'You might be in for another surprise.'

Chapter Five

The enormous chandelier lit up the Stockport House ballroom. Dulci cut the air with an experimental slice of her rapier, upsetting the lazy waltz of the dust motes in the streams of light. Satisfied with the balance of her weapon, she slid a button over the point and tossed another button to Jack. 'Too bad we can't put a button on the sharp edge of your wit. Everyone was talking last night about how you fairly skewered Señor Ortiz the night before with your linguistic prowess.'

Jack slid the button over the rapier point. 'Are you defending him, Dulci?'

'Only because you were acting like a dog in the manger.' Dulci took another practice slash.

'I disagree.' Jack executed a lunge against an unseen opponent. 'I was clever and he'd been ogling your bosom far too long to be appropriate.'

Dulci made an arcing slash. 'Is there an appropriate

amount of time for that? Perhaps some kind of hidden gentleman's rule?'

'About bosom ogling?' Jack lunged, stretching his leg muscles, thinking for a moment before responding. 'Yes, no more than two seconds and then one's eyes must revert back to the lady's face and not stray again. That way, she'll wonder if you ever looked in the first place. Of course, if one's partner is especially well endowed in that region and one is very skilled, one can sneak a few more glances by adopting a contemplative look during conversation and drop one's eyes without a move of the head. But I wouldn't recommend it for everyone, it takes a lot of practice to perfect.'

'That's perfectly appalling,' Dulci scoffed. 'You don't have a rule, you have a whole treatise!'

'Makes one wonder what other hidden rules govern the lives of gentlemen, doesn't it?' A wicked gleam lit Jack's eyes. He raised his rapier in a fencer's salute. '*En garde*, my dear.'

En garde indeed! How was she supposed to concentrate after that? They fell into first position. Jack thrust forwards and Dulci parried with expert ease out of reflex, struggling to drag her thoughts back from the conversation.

Jack made a daring lunge and caught her rapier arm out of position. Dulci tried to recover, but was not fast enough to deflect the strike.

'*Touché*. Round one to me.' He winked. 'You weren't concentrating. Perhaps it was my exquisite physique that distracted you.'

Dulci flashed Jack a withering look and determinedly took up her position. 'I'm just not used to seeing you in such light colours.' In truth Dulci did find it something of a novelty to see Jack in a plain white shirt and tan breeches. Such clothing didn't hide anything and her imagination was embellishing heavily, firing her already active imagination to indecent levels. She'd end up skewered by her own blade if she wasn't careful.

He looked almost normal, standing in her ballroom wearing regular clothing. Except for the fact that there was nothing ordinary about Jack regardless of what he wore. It didn't matter if he was the diamond-buttoned fop or the sombre gentleman, Jack drew people to him by the sheer force of his personality, a unique blend of the light and sharp witted, underneath which lurked a dangerous intelligence that men respected and women yearned to possess.

She was no different in that regard. Dulci wished she could unlock the secrets of his mind. But Jack was a guarded man, a puzzle she had yet to solve, which probably explained why he was standing in her ballroom fencing with her, when she was supposed to be mad at him.

'Are you going to engage any time soon?' Jack drawled, scolding her for wool gathering.

'I was wondering why is it that you're here when I'm supposed to be upset with you.' Dulci took the offensive and pressed him hard with a series of attacks.

'Do you have an answer?' Jack asked with a sharp riposte that bought him back some ground.

'None that I like.' Dulci flicked her wrist and delivered a complicated stroke that nearly disarmed him. She grimaced in disappointment. That move always worked on other opponents. Jack must have wrists of steel to successfully deflect it.

Jack groaned. 'That's hardly a resounding endorsement.'

A smile twitched at her mouth. Dulci felt a laugh coming on that would surely disable her. 'Don't make me laugh, Jack. You're not fighting fair.'

Jack grinned deviously and Dulci knew she had to hurry if she meant to win before she burst into laughter and dropped her guard. Dulci feinted, parried two more quick strokes, then suddenly changed hands. Her left wasn't her strongest arm, but she was counting on the surprise giving her a few seconds' advantage.

This time her tactic worked. Dulci claimed the round four strokes later.

'Nicely done,' Jack commented, graciously ceding the round. 'I underestimated you. I didn't know you'd developed your left arm.'

Dulci ran a towel along the length of blade, wiping it clean out of habit rather than need. 'Turnabout's fair play. I underestimated you in the first round. No one has successfully deflected the move I used towards the end.' Dulci paused, the easy conversation catching her off balance. It was a moment between equals. Eyes met and held. Jack was on the move, crossing the small distance between them.

'You could do better with it. Let me show you a

stronger way to deliver that blow.' Without waiting for permission, Jack slid behind her, his hand covering hers on the hilt of her rapier, his other arm about her waist, drawing her against him as he directed her into position.

The nearness of their bodies swamped Dulci with an acute sense of intimacy. She was so close to Jack she could actually smell him right down to identifying the brand of gentleman's soap he'd used for his *toilette*: an almond scent sold at an exclusive store on Bond Street.

She could identify other things, too: the fact he was five inches taller than she; that she could use the hollow of his shoulder to rest her head and in turn he could use the top of her head to rest his chin; the surprising strength of his arm. Beneath his clothing, Jack possessed a remarkably fit body, built to a fencer's perfection: lean and trim, deceptively muscular, with narrow hips and long legs. An ideal build for stealth and speed, two useful tools an épéeist relied on regularly.

Dulci's face heated at the direction of her thoughts. She was thankful Jack was behind her. She didn't want Jack thinking she could be had too easily like his strawberry actress. Besides, this was all meant to be a purely academic exercise between fellow fencers. But with Jack one could never tell. Jack had the ability to turn the most mundane gestures into a seductive prelude to all sorts of pleasurable sins. After all, they'd only gone out to the garden for a harmless walk.

Jack's hips shifted against her back, his voice soft at her ear in a most non-academic tone. On purpose? Dulci wondered. 'Let's take a step forwards and try it now with the steady wrist, no flicking this time.'

They moved together, stepping and striking. 'There, do you feel how much stronger the blade's position is without the flick at the end? Good. Whoever taught you that was more interested in showmanship than real prowess.

'Now, try it against me.' Jack left her and picked up his own foil. She felt strangely abandoned without the warmth of Jack, the feel of Jack, behind her. Dulci was half-tempted to ask him to show her the move again. The only thing stopping her was her pride. Such a trick was a ploy other women would use. She would not stoop, hard as it was.

Dulci gamely readied herself and engaged. This time the move worked and Jack found himself disarmed in short order.

'Very good,' Jack applauded, his admiration obvious, as was his approval. Overt approval was not something she was used to. Men might admire her, and she knew very well that many did. But admiration was not the same as approval. It had taken her a long time to understand the nuances that separated the two.

Men who considered themselves modern and above the traditions of their station might enjoy privately fencing with her, might take pleasure in discussing her collection of histories and artefacts, might even applaud her personal studies from a distance. All of that was well and good in their minds until it came to marriage. A man could admire such traits from afar, but no man wanted to be shackled permanently to a woman who possessed those traits. It had taken six marriage proposals for her to fully understand.

But Jack was different. She supposed it was because he'd openly declared himself not the marrying kind and she could trust him to stand by that declaration unlike Gladstone, her sixth miserable proposal. Gladstone had declared no more than friendship and respect for her and then surprised her with a marriage offer accompanied by a list of demands regarding the things she'd need to give up as his viscountess.

In those terms at least there was no risk of such a misunderstanding with Jack. She understood Jack perfectly. Rumour could be trusted in this regard: he offered a moment of physical pleasure, no promises attached. A relationship would last only as long as Jack's work didn't encroach. In many ways, a relationship with Jack was over before it started. A woman who gave herself to Jack would have to be happy with whatever she could salvage. In the long term, Dulci doubted she could do such a thing. But it hardly mattered. She wanted only the experience he offered and then they could go their separate ways.

The thought haunted her throughout their work out. Dulci was glad for the excuse of exercise. She could pretend the flush on her cheeks was from their exertions.

They worked a while longer on footwork and various techniques until both were well exercised from their efforts. Dulci stopped and wiped her face with a towel. 'I'm finished, Jack. How about you? I'll have a tea tray sent to my collections room. We can eat a little supper and I'll show you the new batch of artefacts. I've just begun cataloging them. You can see for yourself that I've not been hoodwinked into buying fakes.'

The collection room far exceeded any of Jack's preconceived expectations. Two adjoining drawing rooms had been devoted to Dulci's work, the dividing doors between them pulled back to maximise the space; tall windows overlooking the back garden let in copious amounts of light during the day. Where the light was best, a long work table sat against a wall, strewn with stones, statues and wood carvings. Bookcases were laden with atlases and treatises from the Royal Geographic Society. Free-standing curio cabinets with glass shelves stood about the room, compelling the visitor to wander, stopping to look at each treasure.

And they were indeed treasures, Jack noted, studying each case in turn. It was impossible to tell how honestly anyone had come by the items, but they were authentic. He could rest easy on that account. Dulci had not been misled into purchasing frauds. He stopped to eye a splendid lapis-lazuli-and-gold Egyptian collar. 'These are very fine items, Dulci.'

He studied a cabinet containing a set of bronze elephants with jewelled eyes. 'From India?'

Dulci moved to stand beside him. 'From a maharajah. An old friend brought them back for me a few years ago.'

'Is that wistfulness I hear?' Jack asked, tossing her a sideways glance. 'Would you like to go to India some day?'

'I'd like to go anywhere.' Dulci ran an idle hand over

a mask, tracing the contours. 'India, Egypt, the Americas. There's a big world out there—' Dulci waved a hand '—and I've seen so very little of it.'

A footman entered with the trays and Dulci crossed the room to direct the setting out of the tea and supper on a vacant table. Jack studied her as she gave instructions, her dark hair hanging in a thick braid down her back, the shapely curve of her hips in the tight fencing trousers she wore.

A stab of jealousy went through him. He was an only child and had never acquired an appreciation for sharing. Had Gladstone seen her dressed thusly? Probably not, Jack reasoned. No man could see Dulci turned out in tight trousers and white shirt and blithely let her go. He could feel himself rising appreciatively at the provocative sight of her backside. On the other hand, maybe Gladstone, traditional bastard that he was, had seen Dulci like this and promptly run the other way. Gladstone wouldn't know what to do with a woman like Dulci.

Jack knew. Whether or not that was a credit to him, however, was in dubious question. Dulci was a woman full of passion, a woman ready to burst with it. He recognised it in her smiles, in her blue eyes so full of life. It was there in her dares, those stupid dares that would bring her down sooner or later. She would not be careful for ever. One risk would be to go too far with the wrong sort of gentleman who would covet her *joie de vivre*. He would spare her that humiliation, that fall from grace if he could. But Dulci would not tolerate being reined in.

She'd done an admirable job of fooling London

society so far. He could hardly reconcile the perfectly coiffed Incomparable who took to the dance floor every night of the London Season with the energetic virago who'd bested him at fencing and took a serious interest in anthropology. He supposed it was something of a revelation to learn he wasn't the only one who wore a mask. In that, he and Dulci were quite alike.

The one thing that had become abundantly clear to him in the past few months since Christmas and intensely so in the past few days, was that he wanted her. Kissing her in the garden had only served to re-ignite his previous desire. He wanted all that energy, all that beauty, all that wit, in his bed. He knew too that it would have to be her choice, her understanding of what such an arrangement would mean and what it would not, both for her as well as for him.

There were so many reasons not to pursue this mad passion any further; she was untouched and he had nothing to offer—nothing he *would* or *could* offer. This decision would cost her far more than it would cost him. It would not impede his chances to marry—not that he had any plans in that direction—but it would impede hers should she ever change her mind and accept some erstwhile suitor in the future. But the body defied logic. Such reasons did nothing to staunch his desire.

The supper things were settled at last to Dulci's satisfaction and Jack took a seat on the sofa across from her, picking up the thread of their interrupted conversation. 'If you want to travel, why don't you?' Jack reached for a plate of cold meats and bread.

Dulci laughed. 'I haven't the same freedoms as a man, Jack. I can't pack my maid off to Egypt with me as if it were a trip to Bath.' Dulci bit into her meal with a ferocity that echoed her disapproval of such strictures.

'Of course not. Surely something can be arranged. There are guidebooks and tours these days. You'd hardly be alone.'

Dulci shook her head and made a face. 'I don't want to travel with a tour. It would be incredibly boring, visiting all the same places everyone else visits. I want to explore. You've seen land no Englishman has ever seen. It's simply not fair. You got to because you're a man.' Dulci sighed and sank back against her chair. 'You don't know how lucky you are, Jack. Your life is portable, your body is portable. I wager you could walk out this door and be on a ship to anywhere by the tide, or a mail coach within minutes of leaving my house.'

Dulci's eyes burned with a need so intense Jack felt it sear him deep inside. Shame on society for having no idea or tolerance for such a fire. Inside the walls of her brother's house, she could wear trousers and fence, write her articles, collect her artefacts. But not beyond. Outside Brandon's home, she was trapped by society's rules and by her sex.

'Is that why you haven't married?' Jack took an educated guess. Dulci could no more bear half a life for herself than she could half-measures from anyone else.

'Whatever does that have to do with anything?' Dulci's answer was sharp and defensive. He didn't blame her. His comment sounded entirely *non sequitur*, only it wasn't. He could see the connection. Marriage would take her out of Brandon's house, out of the only place she had any freedom. Jack loved women, but he was heartily glad he'd not been born one. He wanted to say something that would comfort her, but he could not give her empty words. She would know they were just that.

'For your information, I haven't married because I haven't met the right man.' Dulci took a defiant bite. Jack fought a smile. It wasn't anyone who could convey all manner of message by simply eating.

Jack wasn't ready to let the conversation go. It was proving to be far too interesting. 'The right man would be…' Jack let his words fall off.

'Out there somewhere.' Dulci fluttered a hand. Not the answer he was looking for. He'd been hoping for a list of itemised qualities. 'I am in no hurry. I have no reason to marry.' She fixed him with a pointed stare. 'Unlike yourself. What are you now, Jack? Mid-thirties? You need an heir for that new title of yours.'

'Same reasons as yours, I suspect.' The conversation was suddenly not as interesting as it had been. Thoughts of an heir and how they were begot had aroused him. He set down his plate and rose. 'Come and show me the Venezuelan items. It is why you brought me up here, isn't it?' he charmed shamelessly. 'Or is this a new rendition of showing off the etchings?'

Dulci led him to the long work table beneath the windows. The items were laid out by groupings, some already tagged with notes lying beside them. 'These are cooking implements from what I can tell—a *metate*, a pestle.' Dulci reached for a book nearby on the table and turned to a marked page. 'The items match the drawings here and the brief description.' She showed Jack the page. 'I'd like to know more, though. These items suggest a certain diet and they rule out the presence of other foods. One can grind grains and seeds with these, but I have yet to find any tools that would be good for meat dishes. It tells me these people don't eat meat at all or at least very little.' She stopped herself. 'I didn't mean to go on. Am I boring you?'

'Hardly.' He could listen to Dulci talk all day, although given the choice there were other things he'd rather do with her. He'd wanted to see the artefacts but this evening appointment was proving ill founded. Fencing had been quite a stimulating exercise, her body pressed to his as he showed her the appropriate move and she'd not been immune.

Jack was impressed with her reasoning and said so. Dulci shrugged. 'I've picked up many tips from the lectures at the Royal Geographic Society. When they say something like that it seems so obvious, yet I wouldn't have thought of it on my own. It's quite a reminder about how locked into our worlds we get, the blinders we wear without knowing it.'

'Still, your applications of the knowledge are very insightful,' Jack complimented.

'I am hoping Señor Ortiz can fill in some blanks for me, however. The British library was severely deficient in any relevant texts, another reason why I want to do an article,' Dulci said with more enthusiasm than Jack liked. It was the second time she'd mentioned wanting to use the Spaniard as a resource.

Jack had to prevent such a discussion from happening. It didn't matter if this was the same cargo Ortiz was looking for, suspicion on Ortiz's part would be enough. Jack did not want to think what lengths Ortiz might go to in order to retrieve the cargo. But now wasn't the time to dissuade Dulci. He had to choose his moment. Jack picked up a heavy mortar to examine. He ran his hands over the smooth rock surface, an idea taking root. If this was the missing cargo, what would Ortiz be looking for? An artefact with a hidden cavity? If he could find the map first, he could use it to lead Ortiz away from Dulci.

'The tribes Schomburgk and I ran into on the Anegada mission were infamous for their booby-traps. There were all kinds of secret levers and counterweights to spring trap doors and such. Do you think the Arawak have secret hiding places? Have you read of any similar traditions?' Jack kept a certain amount of levity in his tone. He didn't want to appear too eager.

Dulci knitted her brow, making an honest effort at recalling. 'You mean like a false bottom? I haven't heard of anything like that. It would be exciting though, wouldn't it, to find a hidden treasure.' She scanned the assortment of items on the table. 'I am afraid most of these items are too small, and I'd doubt stone is very easy to carve out a hidey-hole in.'

'I suppose so.' Jack assented. Many of the items *did* look too crudely carved from hard stone to hide a secret compartment with much skill. But his eyes silently lit on a wooden statue at the far end of the table and a collection of boxes with carved lids. He'd like to study those further without drawing Dulci's attentions. Maps could be folded. They didn't have to be rolled. Folded, they would take up far less room. A paper map could be folded down quite small.

'A single item contains an entire belief system if one knows how to look at it. This one tells me about their religious preferences. Nature is their god,' Dulci was saying. 'I think this item is almost beautiful.' It was the soft, reverent quality of Dulci's voice that drew his eyes to her and the item she held in the palm of her hand, a fertility fetish. 'It's been carved out of turquoise and someone spent hours polishing it. Perhaps it belonged to a tribal queen.'

The fetish *was* beautiful and highly corporeal with its full breasts and round belly or maybe the moment owed its sensual overtones to Dulci's voice. Jack felt his member stir in response. It had been stirring for the past three days since the first night in the ballroom, if the truth be told. Did Dulci have any idea how she was affecting him? The evening, the delightful company, the temptation of Dulci's fire were overpowering. Perhaps they could play a little without too much harm, Jack's inner devil suggested.

He took the fetish from her. 'Maybe it was a gift from her lover.'

This time there could be no mistaking his statement as an academic assessment. Jack's words were charged with explicit seduction. Something potent and hungry sprang to life between them. Jack let her see his rising need in the slow gaze that caressed her face, in his fingers' deliberate stroking of the little fetish—a move calculated to look absently done. He dropped his gaze down her body. It had the desired result. Dulci bit her lip, stifling a little gasp at his boldness.

'Stop it, Jack,' she scolded, a nervous, excited tremor in her voice. 'That was more than two seconds.'

'I am making my intentions known.' Jack took her hand. 'Don't pretend you didn't see this coming.'

'No, I won't pretend it.' Dulci trembled as he ran his knuckles gently the length of her arm. 'I've wanted it. It's time to finish what we started in the orangery.' Her voice was nothing more than a breathy whisper, her desire getting the better of her.

'And the garden, don't forget.' Jack reached for her, pulling her hard against him for a slow kiss. She was an innocent wanton. 'Do you know what we started?' he whispered, testing her.

'I have no idea, not really.' She parted her lips, wet and wanting. 'But I want to know, Jack. I want to know everything and I want you to show me.' Those blue eyes of hers smouldered with want; every man's fantasy, his fantasy—Dulci in his arms, giving him permission to unleash her passion, to show her what her body was made for. It was a potent, frustrating elixir that worked all kinds of magic, undoing his tenuous grip on the realities beyond this room, this night.

'Do you know what you're doing, Dulci?' he asked one last time. He wanted to be patient, but it was difficult to be patient when one was rock-hard and had been for some time.

'I know, Jack. This is what I want.'

Jack nodded and stepped away from her.

'What are you doing? Where are you going?'

'I'm locking the door. No more interruptions, not for this.'

Dulci waited for him at the sofa, watching him as he locked the door. He was playing for time for her sake, giving her a last moment to make her decision. The die was nearly cast.

It wasn't a question of wanting him.

She did.

It was a question of wanting him enough to live with the aftermath. Not the aftermath of lost virginity—virginity was highly overrated in her opinion, its importance a myth perpetuated by men who didn't want women to have the same freedoms they enjoyed. It would be a relief to surrender hers and have done with it. That was not the aftermath that concerned her. She had grappled with the social implications of virginity since the night in the carriage.

What worried her most in the few moments she had left was whether or not she could let Jack leave as he most assuredly would; whether or not she could stand knowing that something which would mean so much to her would mean so little to him, certainly not enough to stay. It was the way she wanted it, but she was not naïve enough to believe the event would carry no emotional weight for her.

Jack turned from the door and faced her. This was her last chance. She could call a halt or continue with an encounter that would satisfy her curiosity once and for all and hope that it would be enough.

Chapter Six

~~~~~~~~~~~~~~~~~

She drew a deep breath and squared her shoulders in determination, her decision made. Jack could see the resolution in her eyes. He crossed the room towards her, watching as she reached a hand to loosen her hair, shaking it into a long ebony cascade, and Jack's need ratcheted up another impossible notch. Dulci might be untouched, but she was bold, an undeniably heady combination.

Something flickered in the blue flames of her eyes. Faith, perhaps? Faith that she'd made the right decision, faith in him that he wouldn't fail her? She wrapped her arms about his neck and he pressed her against him, covering her mouth with his in a full-bodied kiss.

The dance had begun. He would start slowly, letting their bodies know one another and then…well, then he would take them both to pleasure. He sensed her impatience, her curiosity. 'Patience, Dulci. I'll get us there, but not too soon. The journey's half the fun. You'll see.'

* * *

His hands teased her breasts through the fabric of her shirt, a hand slipped down to cup her through the trousers at the juncture of her thighs, making the presence of clothing seem as erotic as being without. Jack made short work of her shirt fastenings and she changed her mind. His hands worked magic on her bare skin.

'I thought massages were for backs,' Dulci observed languidly, her body boneless beneath the soft caress of his thumbs high on her rib cage, tantalisingly close to her breasts.

'Only for those of a limited imagination, my dear.' Jack lowered his head and kissed her belly. A hot shiver shot through her and Jack gave her an iniquitous smile. 'That would be like saying kisses were only for the mouth, don't you think, Dulci?'

'You're a wicked tormentor, Jack.'

Jack merely chuckled and did away with her trousers, his hands sliding up the bare skin of her legs. 'I love your legs, Dulci,' he murmured, stopping to kiss the inside of her knees and stopping again to kiss the inside of her thighs. 'They're so lithe and so very long, supple enough to wrap around me, you can hold me tight when I am deep inside you.'

His hot eyes shot up to her face, full of want and anticipation, reminders that the pleasure the two of them invoked now was a prelude to the mysterious pleasure yet to come.

Then it was his turn. He moved apart from her and

undressed swiftly, letting her look upon him. 'Would you like to touch me, Dulci?'

She nodded, letting him take her hand, guiding it between his legs, to where he wanted her hand the most: on him, at the core of his manhood. He held her there, showing her how to stroke him fully, how to tease the tender tip of him. Dulci was in awe. These were glorious secrets.

He stopped her hand. 'You'd be the death of me if I let you, Dulci. But there's more to come. Let me show you.' He gently pushed her back against the sofa cushions.

He drew a deep breath and lay over her, covering her with his length. She could feel his strength in his reserve; the effort he took not to burden her with his full weight, the power of his erection where it lay between them prodding at her entrance. Jack was kissing her again, taking away any ability to think, reminding her now was not the time for reflection but for action.

She shifted her hips in intuitive welcome and Jack took her in a quick, thorough thrust, tearing away the thin proof of her virginity. She gasped. Jack stilled inside her. She stretched around him and then they plunged together, meeting each other in the ancient mating waltz, finding the exquisite rhythm that pushed them towards brilliant fulfilment. Her legs locked about Jack, holding him deep, her body feeling each intimate tremor as he neared his completion, shattering inside her while she shrieked her own satisfaction, oblivious to the fact that though locked doors can keep people out, they can't always keep sounds in.

* * *

It was a while before she wanted to talk again. In the aftermath of their love-making, all she wanted to do was lay on the sofa with Jack, somnolent and satisfied. Somewhere in the depths of the house a clock struck the late hour. The evening had fled. It was now technically morning. It seemed surreal that balls were still going on all over town. That world seemed irrelevant and far away compared to the world she and Jack had created here.

But this could not last and she knew it. Still she could not willingly rouse herself. Not even reality could compete with being tucked against Jack's naked warmth, his sex stirring already against her buttocks, his voice teasing in her ear. 'What shall we do for an encore, my dear?'

'I have an idea,' Dulci whispered, moving to sit astride his thighs, fully ready to give herself over to a night of decadence.

In the early hours of the morning, another idea occurred to her, surfacing from the warm depths of replete desire. Maybe this was why she hadn't found the right man. Who could possibly give her the pleasure she'd found with Jack? Sexual pleasure, certainly, but there was another level of pleasure, too; their sharp repartee in the ballrooms, the other exchanges, too, like when they'd been fencing, when their mutual guard was down. All of that would disappear when she married. No man let his wife keep any male friends she might have acquired previous to him.

Probably for this very reason, Dulci thought, snuggling a bit closer to a dozing Jack; fear that his new bride had a lover prior to him, which in turn created an awkward, competitive triangle. No man wanted to worry about living up to past comparisons, especially if that comparison involved Jack.

Unless that husband was Jack, came the unbidden, forbidden thought. The thought was shocking, a violation of what she'd promised herself with regard to Jack: expect nothing beyond the moment, *want* nothing beyond the moment. He would not stay and this had been about curiosity only.

She must have tensed. Jack murmured in his sleep, his hand warm where it lay splayed across the flat of her stomach.

Jack was self-proclaimed non-husband material and Dulci couldn't disagree. Jack as a husband only *seemed* like a good idea in the aftermath of their passion. It was probably natural to entertain such thoughts. But it wouldn't always be like this. She knew empirically that outside the passion, outside the body he shared to its fullest in bed, there were times when he'd be gone and things he could not share when he returned. She would only ever have part of him. The trail of women he left behind him was testimony enough in that regard.

Needing to distract her mind from such errant and dangerous thoughts as marrying Jack, Dulci rose from their makeshift bed on the floor, the sofa having been outgrown by their antics hours ago. She draped a burgundy throw about her shoulders and went to the work table. Jack groaned his disappointment behind her.

'I'm looking for something I want to show you.' The throw slipped down one bare shoulder as she shuffled through the objects on the table.

'I like the view from here,' Jack murmured appreciatively.

'You're insatiable,' Dulci scolded, but she didn't mind. His comment warmed her on the inside. There was a certain pleasure in knowing she was an equal match for her lover's enthusiasm.

Lover.

It was the most apt term for describing Jack. He was her lover. Nothing more and certainly nothing less, if she were entirely sanguine about it. After last night, they now existed in an erotic limbo between merely slaking physical needs with the other and something more philosophical, more committed. What would it be like to meet in society after this?

Above the work table, the long windows captured the moonlight. Evening had become night.

'Aha! I found it,' Dulci crowed triumphantly, making her way back to him.

Jack levered himself up on one arm. 'What treasure is this, Dulci?'

She sat down beside him on the floor and slid in close. 'It's a journal. Vasquez brought it in the last shipment.' Dulci flipped open the worn leather book. 'The drawings are very detailed. I thought you might recognise some of the things from your trip.'

'Is this a gift?' Jack teased.

'Sort of. I haven't read it yet,' Dulci began. 'It has

occurred to me that it might be a good source of information regarding my artefacts. Perhaps I could pass it on to you when I'm finished?'

Jack reached for a strand of her hair and twisted it about his finger. 'It's a lovely gift, Dulci. You may use it as long as you wish. It's like giving someone a book from the lending library as a present, though, if you think about it,' he joked but she could tell he wasn't offended.

Dulci snuggled down against him. She could feel his eyes moving over her shoulder, taking in the pages illuminated by the fading light. Dulci reached for a nearby oil lamp and dragged it to a low table closer to them. She turned up the wick. 'Now you can see better. There's all manner of information in here, birds, plants, even maps, Jack.'

Dulci flipped through the book. Jack offered a comment here and there, but it was becoming exceedingly obvious he was more interested in the warm woman curved against him and the flame-lighted intimacy of their situation. Then something on the pages caught his eye and the hand absently stroking her hip stalled in its lazy motions. 'Wait, Dulci. Go back a page.'

'What is it? Did you recognise a place?'

'The page is creased awkwardly by the book spine.'

Dulci ran her hands along the place where the spine met the page. 'You're right, Jack. The page unfolds into a larger page.' Dulci unfolded the sheet and another carefully folded sheet fluttered out.

Excitement seized Dulci. She scrambled to her feet,

eager to lay the new paper out on the table, Jack following close behind.

Dulci lit another lamp at her work table, illuminating the place names and the land contours. Dulci traced the lines of rivers, pronouncing their names, 'Orinoco, Cassiquiare, the Amakura, the Essequibo.' She paused. 'This is a map of British Guiana. These are the rivers that form the boundaries with Venezuela. The Arawak live along here.'

Excitement thrummed through her. This would help her research immensely. She turned to look at Jack. 'Do you know what this means?'

Chapter Seven

Oh God, did he know. It meant the rumours were right. There was a forged map. More than that, it meant Dulci was in great peril. He could no longer pretend her cargo wasn't the cargo Calisto Ortiz was looking for. The map made it a certainty. Still, there was one more test the map had to pass.

Jack held his breath, his suspicions high despite the plea that ran through his mind like a litany: *Please don't let it be the map.* But he was almost certain it was.

In the dim light, the map looked remarkably accurate based on his knowledge of the region. Jack leaned forwards and scrutinised a faintly darker line along the Essequibo that shouldn't be there. Based on currently recognised boundaries between the two territories, this map was a fraud.

Jack tamped down his fears. His imagination was running away with him. There was nothing to fear yet. No one knew Dulci had it yet. No one even remotely suspected she had it and no one would as long as she didn't tell Señor Ortiz she had recently purchased arte-facts or that she did business with a Señor Vasquez.

'What is it, Jack?' Dulci queried at his silence.

'Nothing,' he lied swiftly, placing a light trail of kisses on her shoulder where the blanket had slipped again. With one hand he pushed back the heavy weight of her hair, exposing her neck, his kisses moving upwards. 'I was just thinking how much I'd rather explore you than a sheet of paper.'

Dulci turned in his arms, ready and eager in the wake of her excitement over the map. Jack hated himself. Never, ever mix business with pleasure. That was one rule he never broke. He ought to make his excuses to Dulci and track down Gladstone right away. But for the sake of business, he couldn't risk Dulci, in her excite-ment, telling Calisto Ortiz about her discovery during casual conversation on the dance floor. There were things he couldn't risk for the sake of pleasure either, such as Dulci's wrath at another interruption. In the wake of the débâcle in the garden, she would not under-stand another abrupt departure. Especially now their relationship had somewhat changed.

Dulci reached between his legs, duplicating her earlier actions with a smile on her face. Jack groaned in expec-tation. He had to have time to think: what to do about the map, about Dulci. For now, the rules could go to hell.

Calisto Ortiz lifted his tumbler in a silent toast. He reclined against the leather comfort of his chair in his expensive suite of rooms. He took a sip of the excellent liquor, savouring its mellow tastes. Tonight, he was well satisfied and in good humour with the world. Vasquez had been found, questioned and dispatched. And he, Calisto Ortiz, had the answers he wanted. In a vain attempt to save himself, Vasquez had told his captors who had bought the journal. Ironically, such an admission sealed the importer's fate.

Dulcinea Wycroft.

Calisto swirled the liquid in his glass. It was about as pleasant as surprises got. He'd not perceived the beautiful woman's interests went that deeply. Retrieving the map would be delightful and, with luck, there'd be no more need for another murder. Lady Dulcinea would have no idea what she possessed. Women had no head for politics and maps. All he had to do was gain access to her home and ask her to show off her collection. That should not be difficult. Surely she hosted an 'at home' like other women he'd met here in London and surely, like other women in London, she found him charming enough for an invitation to call. It would be the work of a few seconds to pocket the journal during a well-placed kiss. A little flirtation and his plan would be back on track. Ah, yes, after a rough time, there would be some luck at last.

Two nights later at the Mayfield ball, the easy attitude Ortiz possessed was being severely tried. Dulcinea Wycroft had disappeared from society, making it rather difficult to pursue his plan to seduce the journal from her. He was not a patient man. He nodded politely to a passing group that stopped to exchange pleasantries, hiding his growing impatience. Where in the world was Dulcinea Wycroft?

Where the hell was Wainsbridge? Gladstone checked his watch for the third time on the perimeter of the Mayfield ballroom. He dared not check it again. It was unseemly for a gentleman to glance at his watch too often at a ball. Such a preoccupation with time suggested he was only waiting until he could politely move on to the evening's other entertainments, hardly an endearing endorsement of one's hostess and Gladstone was careful not to upset hostesses.

Gladstone was getting impatient. He had news to share. He'd rather have shared his news in a more business-like setting, but time was short. He had not seen Wainsbridge in two days. It didn't help matters that Dulci had been absent from the usual circuit of entertainments too. Their mutual absence raised all nature of jealous conjecture in Gladstone's mind.

Four years ago, he'd made the delectable Lady Dulcinea an honourable proposal of marriage, knowing himself to be an entirely acceptable match for her. She'd refused him, left London quite suddenly in the dead of winter and turned up at her brother's home where Wainsbridge had also coincidentally taken up residence a few weeks prior.

It all looked very suspicious to Gladstone, who could not fathom why Dulci Wycroft would turn him down unless there was another. That the other was a man whose only title had been *earned* through actual *work* and not inherited from the efforts of earlier generations, rubbed salt in Gladstone's wounded ego.

Gladstone glanced about the ballroom, which seemed reserved in its atmosphere tonight without the presence of London's most sharp-witted bachelor and the Season's reigning beauty. Others appeared to sense the difference too. A few columns over, Señor Ortiz, whom Wainsbridge was supposed to be watching, appeared bored with the conversation about him. Every so often, Gladstone noticed the man's eyes drift over to the doorway then, disappointed, drift back to the group surrounding him, many of them women interested in testing the hypothesis of Spanish virility against the real thing.

Volume at the entrance rose suddenly. Gladstone resisted the temptation to look that direction. He kept his eyes fixed on Señor Ortiz, gauging the man's reaction to determine who had walked in. Ortiz's eyes lit up. Gladstone turned slowly to confirm his guesses. Already surrounded by admirers, Wainsbridge and Dulci Wycroft sailed into the ballroom, together, utterly beautiful. There was no handsomer couple in London. It was as if a great spark had been lit. The dancers whirled faster, the music's tempo was livelier, the laughter of the guests less brittle. Was it his imagination or did Lady Mayfield, the hostess, breathe a little easier?

Gladstone moved towards them, anxious to speak with Wainsbridge.

* * *

Dulci saw him coming with a sinking heart, her euphoria over the past two days disappearing with each approaching footstep. It didn't help that she knew it would be like this. Knowing didn't make it any better. She had hoped…oh, how she'd hoped. Gladstone shouldered his way through the crowd with none of Jack's consummate ease, stepping on feet, proverbial and otherwise. A subtle unease crept slowly through her at the determined set of Gladstone's very square jaw and intent grey eyes. Reflexively, she tightened her light grip on Jack's arm.

'I don't think he's here for you, m'dear,' Jack murmured, detecting Gladstone's less-than-discreet progress towards them. 'Tonight, it's me he wants.'

His words were an effective killjoy. Dulci knew what he meant. Back to work. Their sweet interlude was over, and if not over, then definitely on hiatus. When Jack 'worked' he disappeared for stretches at a time. He might surface after a few days or it may be months before he rejoined society. No one knew where he went or what he did until afterwards and then only in vague snatches. Whatever he did, he had done it well enough to earn the accolade of viscount. His services were viewed as valuable to his monarch and to his country.

'Lady Dulcinea, you're looking ravishing tonight.' Gladstone bowed over her hand, his eyes lingering on her face in his usual annoying manner, searching for any sign of affection.

'Gladstone,' Dulci answered with stiff politeness.

She dare not give him even the slightest of polite encouragements. After four years, he'd proven to be the most tenacious of all her would-be suitors. Her quiet rejection had not resulted in the desired effect. If anything, the rejection had made him more persistent.

'Wainsbridge, I'm hoping I might have a private word with you.'

'And I am hoping Lady Dulcinea will favour me with a dance.' Jack's eyes twinkled with mischief. 'What do you think our odds are of both of us getting our wishes?' Those around them laughed. Gladstone narrowed his lips into a grim line, unamused at Jack's light humour.

Dulci did her duty, masking her immense disappointment. 'Wainsbridge, go on with Gladstone. I am sure Lord Gilmore can admirably dance attendance on me until your return.' She smiled at young Gilmore, who seemed overwhelmed by the honour she was bestowing on him.

'Very well, it's all been arranged, Gladstone.' Jack shot Gladstone an ungrateful glare. 'I believe there's a library just down the hall that will suit our purposes. If you'll follow me?'

Dulci fought the urge to follow Jack with her eyes, but that was the behaviour of a besotted fool in love. She dare not give the gossips any grist for their mills. People accepted that she and Wainsbridge might occasionally be seen together because of his friendship with her brother and long association with the Wycroft family. Their clever wagers and sharp humour ensured people believed them tenuous friends at best, two persons who would not have sought the other out if it hadn't been for

Brandon Wycroft, which had been somewhat true until that evening in the orangery. Dulci had no desire to change society's perception. She did not want anyone speculating about the true nature of her association with Jack, especially not now that she had something truly scandalous to hide. How could anyone understand it, this need that drove her towards him? She hardly understood it herself.

So she danced with Gilmore, and then with Carstairs's son, being sure to avoid his feet whenever possible; when she couldn't, she assured him he hadn't hurt her toes in the least. She managed to laugh, to lightly flirt, to drink the punch they all brought her, and to avoid looking at the ballroom door in the hopes that Jack would come sailing back through when she knew very well that he wouldn't.

Shortly before midnight, Dulci contrived a moment alone and escaped the hot ballroom for the cooler locale of the verandah. The verandah was nearly deserted; most couples were inside dancing the supper waltz and making preparations to go into the late-night meal. Tonight was far different than the setting she'd found herself in the previous night. And far less enjoyable. The last few days had been a whirlwind of experiences and it felt good to get away by herself for a moment. She was still reeling from what had transpired with Jack. It was amazing society couldn't tell the difference. She *felt* different. But apparently all the changes were internal. There was no external proof of her escapade.

Dulci found an empty chair and sank into it, grateful for the respite. Pretending lightness and happiness when one felt neither was deuced hard work.

She closed her eyes and slowly plied her fan. She drew a deep, cleansing breath and expelled it. That was better. She had known it would come to this with Jack, this disappearing without any warning. She'd known it could come at any time, two weeks from now, or the moment they stepped back into Society, as indeed it had. Knowing didn't make it easier to accept. Neither did knowing he'd made her no promises. She couldn't be angry with him for breaking what had never been.

'I do not think he's coming back tonight.'

Dulci's eyes flew open at the sound of the accented voice, soft and close. 'Señor Ortiz!'

'I have startled you, Señorita Wycroft. That was not my intention.' He pulled up a small chair and settled himself on it. 'A lovely woman should never be disappointed by a man. I think you would find many of us would fix our attentions on you more firmly than the viscount's divided ones.' He reached for her gloved hand lying in her lap, and traced a pattern on the back of her hand.

Calisto Ortiz was handsome and intuitive, a deadly combination when it came to a woman's virtue. Dulci recognised it immediately. Jack carried the very same qualities. But with Ortiz, she found herself to be immune.

'One can only be disappointed if there are expectations to be met in the first place.' Dulci smiled coldly, retracting her hand, making sure her message was clear.

'I have no expectations of Wainsbridge. Ergo, I cannot be disappointed by his abbreviated attentions.'

Ortiz was not deterred. He merely gave a Latin shrug and sighed. He sat back in his chair and ran a hand through his dark hair. 'Ah, so that's how it is with Wainsbridge. He is a man who keeps his work as his mistress. What called him away tonight? Was it business with a ship? A new cargo? Investments? Perhaps a new property to consider?' There was an insult in the enquiry—the idea that a real gentleman had no work.

Dulci shrewdly assessed the Spaniard, careful not to give away too much with any admissions. He was flirting for a purpose and he had boldly guessed far too much about her and Jack. What did he want? Revenge for the insult Jack paid him a few nights ago? She would not know if she turned him away. Dulci rose and smoothed her skirts. 'The Mayfield gardens are decent, Señor, and their roses are considered quite fine. I could show you, if you wished. Do you grow many roses in Venezuela?'

'I would love a look. I am an avid botanist myself when I am home. I have an extensive greenhouse.' Ortiz offered his arm. 'Is Wainsbridge a botanist?'

Dulci laughed, a real laugh this time, nothing like the laughter she'd conjured up to please her dance partners. The very idea of Jack puttering with rose clippings in a hothouse bordered on hilarious. Jack could not be caged by walls. His greenhouse was the whole wide world.

Chapter Eight

The library was dark and empty, a stark contrast to the vibrant ballroom. A small lamp burned on the fireplace mantel, offering the only light. Jack shut the door and clicked the lock into place. 'What do you need that could not possibly wait?' He began.

'I would watch your tone with me if I were you,' Gladstone grumbled, making his way to the sofa. 'You're supposed to be tailing Ortiz. You've abandoned your post. I shudder to think what you've been doing instead.' But it was evident Gladstone had a pretty good idea. He spat in disapproval, anger and envy etched into every word.

Jack did not care for the man's insinuation, no matter how true in fact, but not true in emotion. What he'd done was certainly not as despicable as Gladstone implied. There was no shame in what had transpired between he and Dulci. There was no dishonour in honest sex between a man and a woman.

Even in the dark, Jack could find Gladstone's lapels. He gripped them, hauling Gladstone to the wall. 'You will not impugn Lady Dulcinea's honour with such disgraceful aspersions.'

'You forget yourself, sir,' Gladstone growled, struggling in Jack's grasp.

'I do not forget a woman's honour, which is more than I can say for you.' Jack let go and stepped back. He'd like to pummel the man with his fists for the crass thoughts. 'Do you have real news, or is this one of your jealous ploys?'

If there was nothing to report, Jack *would* pummel the man, all thoughts of propriety and decorum be damned. He'd been disappointed to be pulled away from Dulci so soon. He'd known it would happen but he'd hoped for a dance or two before Gladstone caught up with him.

They'd had two private days together, two days of protection for Dulci while he thought it all out, although she didn't know that. He couldn't risk not connecting with the outside world any longer. He needed to learn what might have occurred during his absence. Lacking information left him less capable of protecting her.

Gladstone shrugged, straightening his jacket. 'As it happens, I do have news. While you were "otherwise engaged"—' he gave Jack a hard look '—a Spaniard was fished out of the Thames with his throat cut, a nasty piece of work.' Gladstone ran a hand over his mouth as if remembering the ghastly corpse.

'Normally, I'd not pay attention to such a crime, unfortunate as it is. Bodies wash up all the time from suicides to murders. But this man had been beaten long before his throat was cut and whoever did the job left a piece of identification on him. Either the murderer was not cautious or simply didn't care. I think it was the latter, suggesting that the man didn't live in England but was only visiting. The man was too far from home for anyone to come looking for him—'

'Well?' Jack interrupted impatiently. Gladstone was a tyrant when it came to detail and it showed in the man's storytelling. 'Who is the man?'

'Señor Domenico Vasquez, who, we've discovered, rents warehouse space in Southwark.' Gladstone paused to let the information settle.

'The warehouse I trailed Ortiz to.' Jack's insides roiled. He fought to keep his outer façade collected. 'I doubt there are two Spanish importers renting space in Southwark.' Jack spoke solemnly. 'It appears we have a match. Calisto Ortiz is a murderer.'

'We have a *likely* suspect. I doubt he did the actual killing in any case,' corrected Gladstone.

Anger over Gladstone's excessive caution fired Jack's temper. 'Make no mistake, Gladstone, this was not an accidental death. If he was beaten first, it was not a quick crime, done in the heat of the moment by a surprised cut-purse who didn't mean for things to go so far.'

Gladstone looked slightly offended. 'No doubt you're in a position to know such things with all your vast experience.' His tone was not friendly and Jack knew he'd inserted a veiled jab at what he viewed as Jack's inferior birth.

'Vasquez's death confirms much, Gladstone,' Jack said sharply, choosing to let the insult slide. 'Vasquez was in possession of something dangerous, something Ortiz did not want disclosed. We cannot ignore this.'

Gladstone scoffed. 'I must caution you, Wainsbridge, not to be so hot headed. We don't have any proof that Ortiz committed the murder, only that Vasquez is dead and Ortiz visited the warehouse.'

'Connect the damned dots,' Jack growled in disbelief. 'The Venezuelan delegation comes to town followed by rumours of a potential land swindle and the importer is killed on whose ship the cargo in question was suspected of vanishing. The connection seems obvious to me.'

'Señor Ortiz is a Spanish nobleman, he deserves the courtesies one gentleman extends to another,' Gladstone said severely. 'We must tread carefully here in order to avoid creating an international incident. Of course, I don't expect you to know anything about such a code.'

'It sounds quite similar to honour among thieves,' Jack ground out. 'At the very least, we should have Ortiz questioned.'

'Definitely not, it would expose our hand. Then the delegation would know we suspected unfair dealings on the land negotiations.'

'They'll know eventually when we confront them.' Jack thought of the map, but now was not the time to tell Gladstone. He would wait until everyone met together tomorrow to share the map. 'Besides, there's a chance that knowledge could be leverage with Ortiz.

The others in the delegation may not know he's attempting to pass off a forgery as the real thing.'

Gladstone's voice was solid. 'Wainsbridge, we do not take chances. That is an uncalculated risk at the moment.'

Very well. If Gladstone would not take action, Jack would take his own measures. 'Then our conversation is over, Gladstone. Thank you for your news.' Jack gave him a short nod and left the room, his strides long as he hurried his return to the ballroom and Dulci. Gladstone was an over-cautious fool. All evidence pointed to Ortiz's guilt and Gladstone was more interested in extending gentleman's courtesies. Such courtesies made no sense when they put a murderer on the dance floor, able to strike again if he should uncover another link in the chain leading to the map.

Jack re-entered the ballroom, scanning the floor for Dulci. He spotted Lord Gilmore leaning against a post alone and made his way to the young man's side. 'Have you lost her already, Gilmore?' he said with an insouciance he didn't feel.

Gilmore looked shocked at the insinuation. 'She needed a moment to herself, Wainsbridge. She went out on to the verandah.'

Jack moved off, eager to reach the verandah. He was glad to see it fairly empty; spotting Dulci would be easy. Then he looked beyond the railing out into the garden. Good lord, Dulci was out there. *With him.*

Suppositions raced through his mind. How much had Vasquez disclosed before he died? Had Vasquez given Ortiz a name? Did Ortiz know already that Dulci possessed the map? Jack prayed he did not. Damnation, ballrooms had become dangerous places.

They'd also become confining. Jack chafed at the limitations his circumstance placed on him. The primal man in him wanted to rush out into the garden and drag Dulci away from Ortiz. But he could not do so without staking a public claim to Dulci, a claim he had no right to entertain. Dulci would not forgive him. And he had no wish to end up like Gladstone: a jilted, grieving suitor. It came as something of a shock to realise just how much the two days he'd spent with Dulci had affected him.

It had started purely as a protective gambit to keep her out of the public eye. The diplomatic front would not go unmanned in his short absence. Gladstone was out there, after all. But reality had become distorted in Dulci's arms, time a fluid, infinite entity, the concerns he lived with daily suspended and surreal in the wake of passion invoked by their love-making. There'd even been times he'd forgot about work entirely, an absolute first for him.

A few couples strolled passed him on the verandah. Jack nodded, but did not encourage prolonged conversation. If the best he could do was play guardian from the steps, then he'd do it with diligence.

A diligence that stung, Jack reflected. It was deuced hard to play the neutral watchdog. They were too far away for him to hear what they said, but he could see them. He could see Ortiz bend close to whisper something to Dulci. He could see Dulci give her head a coy toss.

She stole his breath with the simplest of moves. How had she got under his skin so completely, so entirely? Really, the effect she was having on him was quite unprecedented in his experience with women.

Now that he'd come up for air, had had time to think more objectively about what had transpired between them, he had to wonder—what in sweet heaven was he doing with her? Brandon would skewer him if he knew what his best friend was doing with his sister. But whatever Brandon would do to him for dallying with his sister, it would be far less than what Brandon would do if Jack ever tried to marry her and pull her into the murky instability of his life. Brandon wanted more for his sister than being dragged from peril to peril in the New World, title or not.

Of course Jack *couldn't* marry her. He wasn't a marrying man. His work for the king made any kind of real marriage impossible. Jack couldn't imagine not being able to tell his wife where he went or what he did. The only option was to take a wife who wouldn't care. Since he couldn't fathom *that* cold arrangement, he was left with the last option: not marrying at all.

And if he couldn't marry her, he shouldn't have done it at all. Certainly, Dulci had been adamant in her desires, but he was the one with all the experience. He knew the rules when it came to ladies and maidenheads. Surely he could have stopped their foray into passion's realm if he'd wanted to. There was the rub.

As good as it had been, he was plagued by a twinge of guilt. The bottom line was not pretty: he had seduced his friend's sister. No, not *seduced*. Dulci would never stand for that. Rather, he'd taken his friend's sister's virginity. Never mind that she'd wanted to give it. He was supposed to know better for both of them…and yet he hadn't.

This was just a unique case of unmitigated lust. Dulci had not professed undying love for him and that was for the best. For the time being they were well suited. When the time came to move on, go their separate ways—and it would, he was certain—they'd have no regrets.

That's what he told himself anyway. In reality it was a bit more difficult to imagine. But it was the best he could do in terms of justifying his actions to his conscience—he *did* have one, even if it was slightly rusty from occasional use. This was lust on both their parts. They'd both satisfied whatever curiosity had spurred them. He wasn't dealing with a lovesick girl. He was dealing with Dulci, who was level headed and knew what she wanted.

It *was* better this way. But for now, it was deuced difficult to stand on the verandah and do nothing but watch the object of his erections…er, affections, out in the garden with a very dangerous man. His only consolation was that if he could see them, they could see him. Jack made himself as obvious as possible, standing at the railing, broad shouldered, his arms folded across his chest, his legs shoulder width apart in a commanding stance. Now, if they would only look.

Dulci looked past Calisto Ortiz's shoulder and smiled, hard pressed to contain a rather sudden burst of elation, unexplainable as it was, at the sight of Jack on the verandah. 'You're wrong, you know. He did come back. It is too bad we did not wager.'

Ortiz chuckled. 'Perhaps you would not have won, *mi querida*. Would you have wagered on his return?' The back of his hand lightly skimmed her arm in a gentle motion Dulci found overly familiar. 'Does this mean I must return you to your escort?'

'Yes, I must not keep Wainsbridge waiting.' Dulci pulled her arm away, grateful Ortiz had too much pride to wait to be asked to return her. A gentleman knew what a lady wanted before she requested it.

Nearing the verandah steps, Dulci saw Jack move towards them. For a man who shunned commitments of the interpersonal type, he was behaving quite proprietarily. Ortiz saw it too.

'May I ask a boon before our erstwhile viscount reaches us? May I call on you? I have heard of your Venezuelan collection and I would be honoured to offer my humble assistance. It is rare to meet a woman of your intellectual refinements. I find it refreshing.' His voice was low, concupiscent in its tone.

Dulci glanced up at the Spaniard, genuinely moved by his comment, if not by the innuendo. How long had she waited for a man other than Jack to appreciate something more than her pretty face? Perhaps she'd been too quick to dismiss Ortiz, overly influenced by Jack's obvious dislike of the man. 'You are too—'

'Late.' Jack's interruption cut across the quiet moment, brutal and blatant, his face wearing a hard look Dulci had never seen. He wasn't looking at her but at Calisto Ortiz, with a deadly intent that went far beyond ballroom jealousy.

'Pardon me, *señor*?' Ortiz challenged.

'I said you were too late,' Jack repeated, his hands flexing at his side.

Dulci felt decidedly excluded. There was something feral and male at work in the garden, something dangerous. She'd not seen Jack like this, the urbane king's man transformed into a warrior, possessed of a primal fierceness.

Out of an instinctive need for self-preservation, she stepped back from them both. Jack would have some explaining to do when she got hold of him.

Ortiz's eyes narrowed. He was assessing, Dulci thought, wondering if he could best Jack in some way and whether or not such a display was worth it. Would it enhance his standing with her even while it created a scandal?

Gentlemen engaged in fisticuffs would not go unnoticed. Jack's green gaze never wavered. At last, Ortiz relented, losing whatever internal debate he'd carried on with himself.

Dulci let out the breath she'd been holding. The imminent danger had passed.

'If you'll excuse us, *señor*?' Jack reached for her, his hand at her back, forceful and strong as if he expected resistance. 'Lady Dulcinea and I have another engagement to attend.'

Curiosity was a powerful motivator, Dulci noted on

the way to the carriage. On any other occasion, she'd have cut up at Jack immediately for manipulating her in such a manner. He'd spoken for her, decided who she would receive and then all but marched her out of the Mayfield ballroom without a word.

A potent silence reigned between them at the kerb while they waited for the carriage. Beside her, Jack stood tall and terse, his eyes habitually scanning their environs. At his side, his hand tapped anxiously against his trouser leg in an impatient gesture. His other hand didn't leave the small of her back.

The carriage arrived and Jack hurriedly ushered her into it, throwing a disgruntled look at the coachman as if to say, 'It's about time.' He didn't relax until they were underway.

'Don't get too comfortable,' Dulci remarked the moment she saw his shoulders ease and settle into the squabs of her excellent seats. 'I'll take your explanation now for your rather boorish behaviour with Señor Ortiz.'

Jack's features still wore the hardness she'd glimpsed in the garden. 'Your importer, Señor Vasquez, is dead. The Thames washed him up yesterday.'

Dulci furrowed her brow, perplexed. Certainly this was a tragedy, but Jack hadn't known the man. It didn't explain Jack's reaction in the garden. 'Dead? How? Was there an accident with his ship?'

Jack's voice was tight. 'No. His throat was cut. It was most definitely an act of murder.'

Dulci fell back against the squabs, her face paling at the thought. 'Why?'

Jack leaned forwards and took her hands in his. 'Someone was after his cargo.'

'Yes, of course,' Dulci said absently. Her mind raced through the conversation she'd had with the man just a few days ago. He'd been nervous, anxious to conclude their business. A horrible thought occurred to her. 'Jack, I have the cargo,' Dulci said slowly, understanding dawning at least in part. 'Whoever killed Vasquez will come looking for me.'

Jack squeezed her fingers and she took comfort from his strength. 'Only if Vasquez gave them a name, my dear.'

It was weak assurance at best. She noticed he said nothing along the lines of 'no need to panic unnecessarily'. Because, of course, there was every need. Dulci knew without being told that there was no way to know what Vasquez had said or didn't say in his last moments. 'In such circumstances, I think we must assume the worst,' Dulci said quietly. 'Tell me everything. Who is behind this and what are they looking for?' She'd meant every word, but she hadn't understood what the worst was.

Jack knew he had no choice but to tell her the truth. 'There's a map with forged boundaries that the Venezuelan government may use to force our hand in the upcoming negotiations over the borders between British Guiana and Venezuela. The map has slipped the possession of its intended owner. It ended up in Vasquez's cargo.'

'Our map,' Dulci stated matter of factly, the pieces of the puzzle becoming clearer. She could see the moment of discovery in her mind, the two of them wrapped in blankets, the firelight, the journal between them, Jack flipping back a page and running his long fingers along the awkward seam of the page. It was hard to conceive of such a simple, intimate moment, playing a critical role in political negotiations.

'Yes, our map.' Jack's face was impassive in the dim interior of carriage. His visage gave away no clue that he shared her images of the map. He was, most unfortunately, all business. Something inside her died and suspicion began to bloom in its place.

Señor Vasquez had been killed for the map. Someone must want the boundaries redrawn badly, badly enough to commit murder. 'What do the lands have that's worth killing for?' Dulci asked.

'I believe there's gold in the contested river valley.' Jack's answer was succinct, direct.

'Do you have any suspects?' Dulci tried to match Jack's business-like tone while her insides churned in anticipation of more bad news.

'Calisto Ortiz.'

Dulci froze, overcome with a morbid chill. The man who'd caressed her arm in the garden, who'd taken dinner with her at the RGS, who'd flirted with her and with whom she'd flirted back, was a murderer. 'How certain are you?'

'More certain than Gladstone. He wants to extend a gentlemanly prerogative to Ortiz and not race to conclusions. I do not suffer from any such compunction.'

'How could I not know?' Dulci was stunned.

Jack shook his head. 'Why should you have suspected anything? You had no reason to think otherwise.'

'He wanted to come see my collection.'

Deceit. A superficial ardour. A kaleidoscope of emotions and motives swirled into hard forms. Nothing was as it seemed. Ortiz had not been interested in pursuing her, but her map. They could not doubt that Vasquez had given him her name. It was the reason Ortiz had sought her out tonight in the garden. If she'd harboured feelings for Ortiz, she might have been hurt by his deception. As it was, she was appalled.

There was a special type of fear evoked from the knowledge of having fraternised with an enemy in such close quarters. That fear was heightened by knowing that the enemy was at large and all secrets were stripped away. There was no longer the protection of shallow façades. She knew now what Ortiz was behind his good looks and easy manners. He knew the same of her. She imagined in his mind she was no longer a pretty belle with whom he could pass his time while away from home. She'd been transmuted from an entertaining interlude abroad to quarry, someone to be hunted and run to ground. If it hadn't been for Jack's interruption this evening, Ortiz would have been easily successful.

Ah, yes, if it hadn't been for Jack... The silence between them in the carriage burgeoned. Dulci took no steps to break it. Earlier suspicions bloomed full in the wake of Jack's disclosures. Jack had been stalking Ortiz from the start.

Façades. Pretences to passion. The kaleidoscope of emotions and motives swirled again, configuring new shapes. Ortiz wasn't the only guilty party here. The difference was that Jack's betrayal hurt. She'd been foolish, believing in Jack's passion, in Jack's promises. Oh, not real promises made with words, but in the promises his body made hers. She'd given herself over to the ridiculous belief that this time it would be different, that she'd be different than the other women he'd been with. And maybe she was. This time she wasn't outside his work like the women he entertained periodically when he was in town. She *was* his work.

The fencing, the desire to see her collection, all an attempt to gauge if she held Vasquez's mysterious, coveted cargo. Then there was the map. He'd known the minute he saw it he'd found the prize, in the middle of an intimate, cherished moment. The following two days—what was she to make of them now? All lies? Perhaps they were nothing more than a delay, waiting to see how events would develop. What promises could she believe? Some of them? None of them?

In all fairness, she'd pushed for the first time, that glorious act of love-making in her work room; she'd wanted that even with the understanding there would be nothing more: no promises, no exhortations of sudden and newly discovered love upon consummation. She'd approached that first time with a judicious eye to reality. But then, there had been more. He'd taken her in his arms and loved her into oblivion, far beyond their initial intentions.

In the two days that followed, she'd started allowing herself to believe things had shifted, that this time, beyond all explanation, it was different for him. She had not realised until now how dangerous that little fantasy had been, how much she'd inadvertently built it up in her mind so that now what he saw as just sex was something she viewed as the worst of betrayals.

'Dulci, say something.' Jack broke into the prolonged silence. 'I understand what a shock this must be.'

The kaleidoscope in her mind stilled, cold objectivity coming to her. She'd heard the rumours about him before, how he seemed utterly devoted and yet possessed the cold-blooded ability to walk away when it suited him without a backwards glance. She'd even been counting on such truths to some extent. She'd wanted no protestations of honour and duty afterwards, no forced proposals more for her brother's sake than hers. Now that she had precisely what she'd counted on, any disappointment she felt was her own fault.

Dulci studied Jack with hard eyes and said simply, 'You're wrong. It's really not shocking at all. It is what I should have expected.'

The carriage pulled into the round drive outside Stockport House. Jack insisted on handing her down, making a great show of searching the area before he let her out of the carriage.

Dulci wished she could sniff at his protective behaviour, but she knew such a gesture was foolish. Whatever she blamed Jack for, she needed him for protection. The one night she wanted to send Jack packing back to his bachelor rooms was the one night she could not risk being alone.

The world she took for granted had become dangerous. How would Ortiz come? This was the most pressing question. His arrival was inevitable. Would he come as a polite gentleman and hope to discreetly lift the map from the collection room? Would he come violently as a thief in the night? Would he stop at that? The other question was how far would he go? Would he assume she was ignorant of what she possessed and leave her alone? Would he assume she understood the value of what she had and seek to subdue her the same way he'd subdued Vasquez?

Dulci walked stiffly to her front door, marshalling her thoughts and her courage. Her motto would serve her well. The antidote for trouble was to expect it and she was expecting quite a lot.

To her dismay, her hand shook slightly with her door key. Jack took the key from her hand and fitted it to the lock.

'I'll have a room readied for you at the top of the stairs,' Dulci said curtly.

If Jack was disappointed in his sleeping arrangements, he didn't argue. 'As you wish, Dulci.'

She wanted him to argue, to put up some kind of protest so she could take it as proof that not all of their passion was a lie, as proof that he understood she was angry with him for deceiving her. But if love-making was on Jack's mind at all, he kept it very well hidden and that infuriated her no end.

Chapter Nine

Calisto Ortiz bent graciously over Lady Mayfield's hand and departed the ball, looking to all he passed like a man headed to the clubs or gambling hells to spend the later hours of the night. He offered no sign of the turmoil seething beneath his well-cultivated surface.

Foiled by Wainsbridge again! It was personally intolerable.

He'd been on the brink, the *very edge* of success! The lovely Lady Dulcinea had been warming to his flirtation, excited by the prospect of sharing her collection with him. Once he'd extracted the invitation, it would have been a simple matter to retrieve the journal and, with it, the map without anyone being the wiser. But Wainsbridge had chosen the choicest of moments to reinstate his curious claim. It did make him wonder precisely what manner of relationship the viscount had with Lady Dulcinea. The man's behaviour spoke of a commitment far deeper than that of a dance partner.

Unless there was another reason for Wainsbridge's possessiveness?

It would be in his interest to uncover who the viscount was and the exact nature of the man's attentions. Perhaps Wainsbridge's interests, like his own, were rooted in something more than the attractions of Lady Dulcinea's pretty face.

Calisto Ortiz stepped out into the night and hailed a hackney, giving directions to a tavern on the Southwark docks. If the viscount was indeed more than an ardent dance partner, he would not have the liberty of waiting to act in a more genteel fashion. Wainsbridge would know what he was after. It was imperative that he act tonight. He knew men on the docks who would gladly perpetrate a break-in. He could not commit such a crime himself, but he could send others to act on his behalf.

The crash of shattering glass woke Dulci shortly after four in the morning, according to the little clock beside her bed. Protection and defence drove her instincts. She pushed feet into slippers, arms into the dressing gown hastily discarded at the end of her bed, her hand snatching up the heavy silver candlestick from a long narrow table as she flew down the hall. There was no time to go for her revolver in the library in her desk drawer. Who would have thought she'd need a gun in her own house?

'Jack!' she called loudly, running past his room, but his door was wide open and he was gone.

Dulci flew down the staircase, her feet certain of their destination: the collection room. The fight was already engaged. Later, when she remembered that night, she'd be glad Jack had got there first. What would she have done against two masked intruders with nothing more than a candlestick?

Dulci gasped at the sight of her beloved room in a shambles. The long windows she adored for their worklight were nothing more than jagged shards of glass, the remnants of the panes laying in a shower of sharp, sparkling rubble on the floor. A few curio cases, which had had the misfortune of being in the battle zone, were turned on their sides, their panels broken. In the middle of it was Jack, shirtless and brandishing a knife she hadn't known he carried. He feinted and dodged, using a curio case as a shield against one of the attackers. Dulci cringed. If only she had her rapier or her gun! But by the time she retrieved either the fight would be over.

Under other circumstances, she might have been riveted by Jack's bare-chested skill, all lean grace in the moonlight streaming through her ruined windows. But the other attacker drew her attention, slinking around to the side of the long work table while Jack was engaged.

Dulci sprang into action, racing towards him. These men would not take a thing from her! Her slippers crunched glass beneath their soles. She brandished her candlestick, swinging it like a medieval mace, screaming a banshee yell. The intruder looked her way in time to see the candlestick seconds before it connected with the side of his face. He staggered backwards into the table and collapsed with a cry.

The cry brought the other attacker. Darting away

from Jack, the masked man lunged for Dulci. In reflex, she put up the candlestick to ward off a blow. The blow glanced off the silver of a blade, but the impact stunned Dulci, and jarred down her arm. She fell, her feet losing their purchase in the glass.

She heard Jack bellow her name, she braced herself for the attacker's assault, but it never came. Faced with Jack, knife in hand, he opted to vault on to the table, making a wild scramble for the window before Jack could pull him back.

Dulci cautiously crawled to her knees, seeing the concern on Jack's face, and beyond him footmen in various states of dress materialising in the doorway. She understood the indecision that flickered across Jack's features. 'Go, Jack! Go after him! I'm fine,' she cried, flinging an arm towards the window. Jack leapt to the table, but he was already too late. The rope jerked away through the window, the attacker having enough wit to destroy the escape route upon reaching the ground.

'The back stairs!' Dulci scrabbled to her feet, running and sliding inelegantly towards the door, Jack behind her.

He seized her in the hall to halt her flight. 'I'll go. Stay here and see to getting our culprit tied up before he wakes.' Jack roughly shoved past her, running shirtless into the night, gesturing to two footmen to follow.

Dulci drew a deep breath, some of the excitement leaving her in the wake of Jack's departure. Jack was right, of course. There was no benefit to both of them haring off into the night. They would come back to find the other intruder gone and the journal with him.

Dulci quickly organised the servants. There were actions to take and decisions to make. Some of them were sent to round up cords from the kitchen. Others were set to watch the captive until he was secure.

Her butler, Roundhouse, asked permission to call the watch. She debated the decision before deciding against it. She also wished to maintain some level of anonymity. She didn't want this break-in announced to the world. Going for the watch would only raise a host of questions. That couldn't be what Jack wanted.

The housekeeper wanted to clean up the room, but Dulci thought it would be better to wait for Jack, for the daylight, and a chance to search for clues. Instead, Dulci set the woman to work making tea and laying out an early breakfast. After a whirlwind of early morning activity, there was nothing to do but wait for Jack's return.

Dulci was dressed and coiffed, looking every inch the respectable young woman by the time Jack came back some time after the clock chimed nine, dressed in someone's ill-fitting shirt with too-short sleeves. It seemed more than hours had passed since the break-in.

She'd never been treated to the sight of a dishevelled, unkempt, sleepless Jack called out in the middle of the night to run the streets of London. The man standing before her in the entry bore little resemblance to the couth, impeccably tailored man who'd squired her to the Mayfield ball only last night. Jack's blonde hair hung in his face, causing him to repeatedly push it out of his eyes. His trousers were ripped at the knees, his chest, where it peeked through the unbuttoned shirt, bore signs of soot and dirt.

She searched his tired face, adorned with dark circles and the blonde stubble of morning beard. He shook his head wordlessly. The intruder had got away.

'Do you want to bathe first or eat?' Dulci solicited.

'Eat, if you can stand me. I'll start with coffee if you have it.' Jack's voice was hoarse with weariness.

'I have breakfast and coffee laid out in the family dining room. I'll send someone to your lodgings for fresh clothes.' She peered closely at Jack. He seemed to sway where he stood. 'Are you all right?'

Jack managed a wry half-smile. 'There's nothing wrong with me coffee can't cure.'

Coffee, a bath and clean clothes did indeed work wonders on Jack. Dulci wondered at his reserves of stamina hours later as he briefed a small team of men, Gladstone included, in the ruins of her collection room, leading them through the burglary.

'There can be no question that the intruders had a specific destination *and* goal in mind.' Jack flashed a sharp look at Gladstone. Dulci recalled Jack's scepticism the prior evening over Gladstone's reluctance to officially name Calisto Ortiz as the prime suspect in Vasquez's murder.

'This room is set at the back of the house and is two storeys from the ground. The intruders came here instead of choosing rooms on the lower level, which would have been accessible with much more ease and without the risk of waking the occupants. It is unlikely someone sleeping on the third floor would have heard a disturbance on the lower level.'

Dulci noted how carefully Jack worded his hypothesis, delicately skirting away from any word that would imply 'we'. Unless called to it, Jack was doing his best to steer attention away from his presence in a bedchamber in an unmarried woman's home.

The three other men nodded their heads, following Jack's explanations. Dulci marvelled at how easily or perhaps willingly the men were led. It was a curious trait of the English to simply ignore what did not please them. If anyone deduced Jack had already been on the premises, no one mentioned it out loud. True to English custom, if it wasn't said, then it didn't happen.

'Did the intruder escape with the map?' one of them asked.

'No, the map is safe.' Jack's answer was direct and short.

'Do we have any idea who sent these men?' asked another.

'*I* have ideas.' Jack shot Gladstone a cool look. 'We have the second intruder in custody. He's been sent to a safe house where he awaits interrogation later this afternoon. I am confident we'll have the answers we seek by evening.'

Dulci hid a shudder. An interrogation sounded exceedingly brutal. She wanted to protest that such extremes weren't necessary, but of course they were. To not extract the needed information from the captured intruder was the height of folly. Was Jack going to do the interrogation? He'd said 'we', implying he and one other. She'd never thought Jack capable of cold-blooded violence. His appearance seemed so immaculate and, well, *clean*, nothing out of place, nothing disturbed by any unruly conduct as if he moved in a world apart from the rest of them. But then, Calisto Ortiz had not looked like a murderer any more than Jack looked like an interrogator. So this was what he did for the king. This was his work.

'Gentlemen, if you'll follow me into the drawing room, there is one more matter we must discuss,' Jack led them down the hall towards the large room at the front. Dulci trailed in their wake, giving instructions to waiting servants that tea should be brought to the drawing room and perhaps something a bit stronger.

'The other item is Lady Dulcinea's need for protection,' Jack began once everyone was settled with tea and sandwiches. He strode meaningfully in front of the long windows, looking out to the busy street beyond the Stockport House gates, all eyes in the room riveted on him.

There was no doubt that Jack was in charge. The unprepossessing Gladstone had faded in to the upholstery of his chair without meaning to. A tremulous thrill darted unbidden through Dulci. There was something undeniably appealing about a man in command, even if that man was Jack and had much to answer for; she'd almost forgot for a moment, but his next words stirred her temper.

'We must operate on the premise that our culprit will try again in the wake of this initial failure to recover the map. That puts Lady Dulcinea at risk. That risk increases if our culprit treats her with the same assumption as he treated Señor Vasquez—that Vasquez not only possessed the map, but knew its purpose.'

She might as well be just anyone Jack was responsible for guarding for all the impassive objectivity he was showing, not the woman he'd lain naked with discovering the dratted map. She wondered what these men might say if they knew precisely the circumstances under which the good Viscount Wainsbridge came across the map.

'The house and Lady Dulcinea must be under surveillance at all times until this situation is resolved.' Jack nodded to one of the men. 'Morrison, I will leave it to you to work out a schedule. I will station myself here as well as much as I am able. We have our jobs, gentlemen. Let's work swiftly and competently; the empire and our monarch depend on us.'

'To say nothing of Lady Dulcinea,' Gladstone said, rising from his chair with a smile that relieved some of her irritability.

'Gladstone, we must be away,' Jack snapped, striding towards them. 'The interrogation, man. They're waiting for us.'

'Might I have a word before you go?' Dulci asked.

'I am afraid not, Lady Dulcinea.' Jack smiled indulgently, coldly. There was nothing of her clever, teasing lover in that smile. 'You can give your daily schedule to Morrison. I'll return later. I will contact your brother unless you prefer to do it yourself. He should be informed.'

The limit of Dulci's tolerance had been reached. Reached and exceeded. She would not stand here and be treated like a hapless female a moment longer. 'Do not mistake me for a schoolroom miss. I appreciate your concern, but I am fully capable of looking after myself. It was me, after all, who knocked out our captive with a candlestick last night.'

'Yes, indeed, Lady Dulcinea,' Jack said through a thin smile. 'I can hardly forget it.'

Jack doubted he'd ever be able to shake the image of her dashing across the room, her pink-silk dressing gown billowing behind her, her hair loose, oblivious to the amazingly sensual image she created, streaks of moonlight turning the thin nightgown she wore beneath the robe gossamer. If it was truly only lust he'd have only noticed the fine fullness of her breasts in that moment. But his thoughts had been obsessed over her safety—how could he protect her when she insisted on putting herself in the centre of the action?

Jack sank back against the carriage seat, not caring that he shared the space with Gladstone. Jack could not recall being this tired in quite some time. Dulci was going to be the death of him. Had she no idea how many times she'd pushed him to the brink of fear last night? The very idea that she'd thought herself capable of taking on a man who outweighed her by at least two stone was enough to stun him, her success at doing so not withstanding.

The remembrance of the man's retaliation was nearly

enough to finish him off. The only thing more frightening than Dulci's 'moonlight charge of the candlestick' against an intruder was seeing the other intruder leap for Dulci, having no scruples about attacking a woman.

Jack, who'd faced down worse than two mediocre burglars, had been scared, not of the act itself; he knew how to handle combat of all nature. He'd been scared because Dulci was at the heart of the risk. He was not used to such an emotion being attached to his work.

What *drove* that fear for Dulci was frightening in itself. He'd worked with partners before and never been frightened for them in such situations. This was not fear invoked by simple lust for another. While he wouldn't name it, he would admit that he felt something stronger than lust for Dulci.

He would not bother himself with the effort of naming that feeling right now. To do so would be imprudent and hasty until he was absolutely sure what that feeling was. Some might rashly name it love, but Jack was unwilling to do so on short acquaintance, both with the sentiment and the woman to whom he might attach the emotion.

Indeed, he wasn't even sure 'love' was the right word or feeling. Just because a man sneezed didn't mean he was catching cold. Then again, a part of his conscience nagged, this might be it, this might be love. If so, it was a deuced rotten time to work that out and he would put off admitting it to himself as long as he could. There was a lot left to work out before his conscience could say 'I told you so'.

In any case, if or when he ever decided to use the term, he would exercise the utmost caution. Love meant promises and he was a man who promised nothing.

All his philosophising could not change the reality of his emotions, which had simmered under the merest veneer of control since he'd seen the intruder lunge for Dulci.

Jack's gut had tightened with rage at the sight and remained clenched with raw, barely leashed anger. That man was going to pay. Jack had followed him into the night, exhausting every lead, every potential, fuelled by his anger. All to no avail. The crafty burglar had gone to ground; his head start out of the window had been enough to elude Jack in London's dark alleys. Jack had returned to Stockport House exhausted and empty handed.

He wouldn't be empty handed much longer. He had every confidence the interrogation would confirm all he suspected. Then he could get back to Dulci. She'd played her part beautifully today in a lovely demure dress of pale blue and lace. No one could have looked at her today and accused her of spending two intimate nights with him. He laughed silently at his mental joke. Dulci did everything beautifully. She couldn't help it. And it had paid off. Her image of quiet innocence and his objective politeness had carried the day. No one had questioned his presence in her home at the unseemly hour of four in the morning.

But Dulci was *angry* and Jack knew he had a reckoning coming. Monarchs and maps aside, Dulci felt betrayed. He knew what she thought; he could have told her sooner when they first discovered the map and he hadn't. He'd wanted to be sure. But he'd waited too long and now she suspected his motives in their brief affair. Well, there would have to be time for sorting that out after… Jack heaved a sigh, fighting the urge to close his eyes. This was an old pattern too in his life. Everything was put off until after. The only problem was that 'after' kept getting pushed further down the line. It was something of a revelation to realise that he wanted 'after' to be 'now' where Dulci was concerned.

'Well done today, Wainsbridge,' Gladstone huffed across from him. Jack did not mistake his opening as a compliment, but merely arched his eyebrow.

'You've managed to avoid scandal.' There it was, Gladstone's real reason for conversation.

'I beg your pardon?' Jack said coolly, pretending to be confounded by Gladstone's reference. If the man was going to bring up certain omissions, he would have to be blatant.

Gladstone's eyes narrowed. 'You were in Lady Dulcinea's house, sleeping in her guest room, I hope, although that hope seems misplaced.'

'Indeed I was.' Jack sat up ramrod straight. 'Lady Dulcinea was in need of immediate protection after you and I met at the Mayfield ball. When I returned to the ballroom, she was in the company of Calisto Ortiz. I escorted her straight home, but I could not leave her. Seeing that she is an old family friend, I saw no harm in staying at a home in which I've been welcomed for several years. It would have been her brother's wish if he'd known she was at risk.'

'You cleverly disguised that today.'

'For Lady Dulcinea's benefit,' Jack said staunchly, rather enjoying putting Gladstone's lurid imaginings to rest. 'Sometimes honourable intentions get lost in social translation. I had no wish for an inaccurate telling to circulate in society.'

'Where I come from, Wainsbridge, when a virtuous woman's honour is compromised, a gentleman does the right thing and marries her, especially if he is party to the compromising in the first place. He knows what needs to be done without society's prompt.' Gladstone took the high ground. 'Then there is no need for a network of lies and half-truths.'

Jack smiled politely. 'Neither I nor Lady Dulcinea have any intention of marrying, each other or otherwise, as I am sure you are well aware.'

Gladstone glowered the rest of the way, but at least, Jack mused, he was silent.

Chapter Ten

More bungling! Calisto Ortiz could hardly concentrate on Adalberto Vargas's words during the afternoon meeting at their leased headquarters, someone's currently unused town house. Vargas was laying out the agenda of their opening discussions with the British. After two weeks of parties and a 'getting to know you' phase, the time to settle down to business had finally come. Much of the business slated for discussion was *de rigueur*, such as the status of the Spanish missionaries along the Orinoco.

In fact, many of these yearly reports were usually handled by the Venezuelan government and the Governor of British Guiana, Sir Carmichael-Smythe. There was seldom a need to bother London with the mundane mechanics of colonial relations. This year, with boundaries in question, it had been deemed more expedient to go straight to London rather than relying on correspondence by steamer.

Such a strategy suited Ortiz perfectly. He'd rather pass off his map of boundaries, drawn by a biased surveyor, among people thousands of miles away who'd never set foot in South America than among people who actually lived there and were somewhat more familiar with the terrain. It would be easier to argue the former boundaries had been flawed, that the river ran at a different angle than the results previously reported.

It was all wishful thinking as of yet, seeing that he didn't have his map to hand. The map was proof that British Guiana had overstepped its physical boundaries. Without it, Vargas could only make polite overtures about 'looking into the situation'. That would take time, years even, given the distance and the expense and organisation of mounting an official expedition. The Ortiz family didn't have years. They wanted to mine the gold *now*, but as long as the territory remained in British hands, all the gold would belong to the British, too, no matter who mined it.

Vargas didn't know about the map. If he did, Vargas would object strenuously. The man was a traditionalist to his core. Calisto had planned on introducing the map on the eve of negotiations, presenting it humbly as a patriotic gift to Vargas. 'Here's a map my family commissioned once of the region,' he'd say simply, adding, 'I do believe it will help your negotiation since it clearly lays out the grounds in contention.' In one short sentence, the map would become valid proof that the territory belonged to Venezuela. Vargas would not doubt the map or even consider that the map might have been the result of money changing hands. He might even get some type of useful commendation for it.

All this could still come to pass if he could get to the map. But now, the risk was greater. Wainsbridge was sure to alert those involved that the map was a fraud and the insinuation that the map was not legitimate would cause Vargas to worry. The intruder Wainsbridge had caught in Lady Dulcinea's home had surely sung like a nightingale under the pressures of the Foreign Office. By now, Wainsbridge knew everything he'd once suspected. But a few well-placed words could mitigate Wainsbridge's claims. That wasn't what worried him.

What worried Ortiz most was that Wainsbridge had turned out to be rather more than he appeared. Calisto's instincts had been correct there.

He idly tapped a finger on the brown folder beneath his hand. The dossier had come before lunch. The viscount actively worked in a quiet but prominent capacity for the king himself. He was also something of an expert on the South American region, having been there with Schomburgk a few years back. Wainsbridge potentially knew too much about the region. He would know what was skewed on the map. He might even guess why. For those faults, Wainsbridge would have to die. Vasquez had died for much less.

Calisto Ortiz smiled with satisfaction. At the other end of the table, Vargas nodded at him, and Ortiz realised Vargas, pompous old windbag that he was, thought Ortiz was smiling at him. There'd been too much bungling already. Ortiz would handle Wainsbridge's demise. He wouldn't personally kill the man with his own hands, of course. After all, why do it himself when there were others who'd be glad to do it for him?

Jack stepped down from the carriage in front of Stockport House, tired and world weary. Dulci had lit the lamps. She'd stayed in for the evening. She'd waited for him. The thought was both comforting and unsettling.

Late spring twilight had descended and the night was mild, a perfect evening for courtship if one didn't have any other pressing matters to consider. Jack always did. It was the trademark of his life now. He took a moment to pause and drink it in. It was quiet here. Stockport House was set back from the street, away from the road noise. One could see the street, but one didn't have to hear it. Crickets chirped in the hedges, reminding Jack of home, the small manor house in the north country where he'd grown up. He closed his eyes. He could smell the roses and honeysuckle planted along the drive and his heart ached for simpler days and simpler pleasures.

It wasn't fair to paint those days as a halcyon past. Those days hadn't been perfect either but this, whatever it was he'd become now, hadn't turned out the way he'd hoped. He hardly knew the man he'd become any more, this man who carried a knife in his boot and interrogated mercilessly. Jack opened his eyes. Enough of that maudlin sentiment. If wishes were horses…

Jack laughed roughly. If wishes were horses, Dulci would be riding pillion behind him, her arms wrapped about his waist, her cheek pressed to his back, her hair streaming in the wind as they charged into the unknown. That was all he'd ever really wanted—someone to share his adventures.

To discover that Dulci was that someone was both hopeful and hopeless. How could he drag Dulci into the wilds he explored? An explorer's life was necessarily devoid of the luxuries she enjoyed without thought. And there were dangers too: disease, hostile peoples, poisonous insects, to name a few. While she might be game for such an adventure, would she be game for what it would do to her life? Unless he married her. That might be the one useful thing to come out of his title—he could make her a viscountess at least. Brandon would have to agree first and Jack couldn't see that happening. Brandon would want more for his sister than a wandering viscount, even if the wandering viscount was his best friend.

Those factors alone were enormous obstacles to his simple wish. They didn't begin to even encompass Dulci's needs or his. How could she love a man she didn't know? He barely knew himself or even if he was capable of love. Certainly he was capable of falling into love. But sustaining it?

Jack climbed the steps and was met by Roundhouse at the door. Roundhouse informed him Dulci was in the garden, Morrison and Tredwick were in the library playing chess, alert to any suspicious behaviour. Two other men were in the garden with Dulci in case anyone attempted to penetrate the house from the garden gate on the alley side.

How much more did Dulci hate him for making her home a prison, a fortress? Stockport House had always been her refuge, the place where she could fence and collect without casting aspersions on her gender. But he'd had no choice. He could not leave the home unguarded. It had been a convenient stroke of luck that he'd been there last night. The consequences of Dulci having discovered the intruders alone did not bear thinking about.

Jack stepped out into the gardens and breathed the fresh night air. He spied Dulci immediately. She sat at a small table, engaged in taking notes from a book. She'd changed her gown again, this time into a simple dinner dress of pale green. Her hair was done in an elegant twist, leaving her neck exposed and delicate. One could not help but be drawn to the single strand of pearls that lay at the base of her neck, innocent and unassuming where her pulse beat beneath them. Jack felt his desire rise. Even in the midst of his exhaustion, he wanted her. He wanted to touch her, to feather kisses down her neck, to feel her body beneath his hands. He would get lost in her and he would be able to forget all else.

'Jack.' Dulci had looked up and spotted him. 'You're back. I thought we'd dine alfresco.' Her greeting was polite, perhaps a bit stiff, wary. There was little warmth to it. She might have been greeting any acquaintance. She made a gesture and servants immediately began setting out dinner trays.

Jack marvelled at the efficiency. Regardless of her greeting, she'd been planning this, waiting for him. That had to mean something. Linen was spread, wine was poured. His plate was filled. Servants disappeared. There was a hardness in Dulci's eyes when she looked at him.

'I would ask you how it went, or how your day was, but that hardly seems appropriate given the circumstances. After all, it isn't as if you're coming home from a hard day's work trying a case.'

Jack raised his glass in a toast. 'Hard work, none the less. No less difficult for its form.' Behind those blue eyes of hers, she was thinking the worst of him.

'Interrogation isn't torture, Dulci,' he said in low tones, careful not to be overheard. 'I gave him a meal and a glass of ale and sat down to talk with him while he ate. That is all.'

'You gave food to a starving man. I am sure he hadn't eaten for a while,' Dulci accused.

Jack sipped his chilled wine. 'He committed a crime, against you. He deserved worse than cold chicken and conversation with me.' He could hear the emotion edging his voice.

'Heaven forbid I should be entitled to a higher sense of justice than other citizens.'

Jack set his wine glass down forcefully, liquid slopping over the rim, his anger breaking loose. 'Did you want me to announce how the map was discovered? Did you want me to say we found it dressed in blankets in between bouts of lovemaking? I had to be objective today. I could not let any of them suspect for a moment that I'd run through London half-naked for you, that I'd been scared beyond belief when the intruder went for you and you fell before I could get there.' Jack paused. 'What do you think would happen, Dulci, if anyone guessed at what we've been doing?'

For once, Dulci had the good grace to look penitent. 'I would not trap you, Jack. I would expect nothing. I would shoulder my part of the blame.'

Jack snorted. 'That would be all of the blame. It's always the woman's fault.'

Dulci chose to ignore him and turned the conversation in an entirely different direction. 'My honour aside, what did you learn today?'

'The man was sent by Ortiz. Everything is as we thought. Gladstone had to eat a small slice of humble pie.'

'Well, then, that's it,' Dulci said with a satisfied half-smile. 'The proper officials know the map is a fake. Even if Ortiz recovered it by some miraculous means, he can hardly introduce it into the talks now that everyone knows. It's over.'

How nice it must be to live in Dulci's black-and-white world. She expected blunt straightforwardness from everyone around her and gave it in return. It was hard for her to conceive of the spaces between where black and white weren't so obvious. Jack's world, however, was a bit greyer. He did not think it was over.

'We must be alert in case Ortiz tries something else.'

Dulci's gaze sharpened. 'Ortiz is not to be arrested?'

'We can't. He has diplomatic immunity. The Venezuelan government can choose to try him upon his return, but we can do nothing.'

'So he's on the loose, able to extract revenge.'

'Possibly. Your safety depends on complete honesty. I will not mince words with you. Ortiz may decide that, as a woman, you should be spared his wrath, that you could not understand the significance of the map.' Jack flashed her a wry smile. 'For once, Dulci, your gender might be the saving of you.'

'You think Ortiz will target you instead.' Dulci divined instantly the hidden message in his words. A flicker of worry flamed in her blue eyes. Jack took it as a good sign. She might be angry, but she hadn't given up on him entirely.

'Yes,' Jack said simply. 'I am sure by now that he has a dossier compiled on me and he knows my background. He's too astute to not take the standard measures. He will know I've been to South America and that should worry him greatly. That I've turned up in the midst of this negotiation will confirm his suspicions. He knows, no matter what you knew or didn't, that *I* knew. I knew what he was after and why he was after it.'

'Then you've come to say goodbye.' Dulci looked away, making a great show of fussing with her napkin beside her plate.

Jack nodded. 'Among other things that need saying.' He gestured to the men walking the garden, motioning they could retire inside. 'Walk with me, Dulci.' He didn't want to explain what was in his heart at the same table where they'd talked of murder and conspiracies.

Dulci took his arm, but she dreaded what he was going to say. In a way, what was to come was far worse than hearing the sordid details of Calisto Ortiz's gory schemes to retrieve a map. 'The hydrangeas bloomed this week.' Dulci pointed to a large pot of blue-and-pink flowers set on the pathway. 'They were late this year. Brandon would have had a fit.'

Beside her, Jack laughed softly. 'Brandon loves to order nature around. Taming the wild suits him.'

'I threatened to let the garden go its own way this year since he wasn't coming to town.' Dulci reached out to touch a petal on the climbing roses. It was nice to talk with Jack this way, without a ballroom of people staring, without innuendo and the double meanings that wrapped most of their conversations. Yet, such a simple discussion seemed surreal. Dulci tilted her head in Jack's direction. 'How is it possible after all that has happened that we can stand here speaking about flowers and Brandon? It's almost too ordinary. My world has been turned upside down and yet it still looks the same, still acts the same. I changed my gown for dinner, I gave orders to the servants, I worked on my notes. Calamity has struck. Shouldn't *everything* be different?'

She studied Jack shrewdly. 'Do you ever get used to it? I am suddenly struck with the realisation that this is what life is like for you on any given day. How do you waltz into ballrooms and make witty conversation every night as if you've nothing more to worry about?' Why hadn't she seen it before, the duality of his life since receiving his title and what it must mean for him? It was more than the secrecy.

'You adapt,' was all Jack said. 'This will pass and your life will return to normal.' He was watching her in that way of his, the heat in his eyes being stoked to life. But there were things that needed to be dealt with before she could fan those coals.

'And your life, Jack?' They moved on down the path to sit on a bench by a statue of a water nymph surrounded by greenery and ferns, water spouting from the jug she carried into a pool of pebbles.

'My life will go on much as it has.'

'You're awfully miserly with your conversation tonight,' Dulci scolded. 'You said there were things that needed saying and yet we haven't said anything at all in that regard.'

'You're the one who wanted to talk about hydrangeas,' Jack reminded her. But she sensed a challenge beneath the scold.

'Maybe that's what we're supposed to talk about,' Dulci answered softly. Jack was leaving, never mind that he'd still be in London. He was leaving her. He would go back to his quarters and he would keep his distance in order to ensure her safety. Then he'd be off on another project for the king. What good could come from talking about other things, confusing things? Maybe she'd be better off remembering this moment with him: a peaceful moment where they'd walked and talked together without artifice instead of clouding it with ambiguous promises.

'You and I are a lot alike, Dulci. We've never been good at doing what we're supposed to. I know what you're thinking, what you're debating in that active mind of yours.' He shook his head. 'Only a coward would let us leave here with nothing more than a discussion of hydrangeas and roses to remember.'

'Jack, you don't need to explain anything. I've got it worked out. I had all day to think.' Dulci tried to stall, tried to protect herself. Jack's eyes were growing darker with desire and, Lord help her, in spite of all her misgivings, her need was rising too, the need to be in this man's arms, to let his strength surround her, to empower her, to forget the danger for a little while.

'I cannot leave knowing that you think what occurred between us was all work, some kind of subterfuge I employed to get to the map.' Jack's voice was at her ear, his mouth nipping gently at her lobe, his hand pushing back her hair. His lips were at her neck now and Dulci arched against him instinctively, wanting to be nearer. It was awkward being side by side, she couldn't get close enough.

'Tell me you know better, Dulci.' Jack breathed heavy and hoarse, dragging her on to his lap, helping her to straddle his thighs. 'Tell me you know our love-making is not an act of artifice. Tell me you know it's honest.'

The desire in his darkened eyes was arresting and potent, the window to his soul open, offering a glimpse into the depths of his character, a swirling mix of the complex and the desperate. Dulci could not deny him; indeed, her need of him was greater because of it.

'Yes, Jack. It's honest,' Dulci whispered, her arms around his neck, her breasts pressed against his chest, her mouth covering his, glorying in the taste of supper's sweet wine. Jack groaned his pleasure, letting her take the kiss where she willed, giving his mouth over to her while he worked pleasure of his own beneath her skirts, hands moving up her thighs, at their apex thumbs gently brushing damp curls, drawing back her secret lips to the tight bud hidden within, one thumb gently skimming until Dulci cried out, begging for a firmer stroke, begging for completion.

But Jack would not relent. 'Let me worship you, Dulci,' he begged, his own arousal powerful and obvious beneath her buttocks. Dulci slipped a hand between them, answering his erotic strokes with delicious strokes of her own, finding the head of his shaft beneath his trousers.

'You're an enchantress, Dulci.' Jack was hoarse, rocking hard against her, needing both his hands to steady himself on the bench. She reached for the fall of his trousers, releasing his hot member, glorying in the fulfilling power of arousing this man to such heights his very control was in question. Tonight *she'd* take *him*, riding him astride in the newly risen moonlight.

Dulci moved to push him back on the stone bench, but Jack had other ideas. 'No, tonight I want to cover you.' His voice was ragged, beyond desire. Dulci thought she heard a new desperation in it. There was wildness in his eyes as he rolled her beneath him, careful of the stone's hardness on her back.

He joined her intimately and immediately, their foreplay having served its purpose, both of them wet and ready when Jack plunged into her. There was no need to be delicate. Dulci didn't want gentle tonight. On that bench, with only nature as a witness, she wanted a release to the madness that raged inside them both. She wanted a release for the anger and despair, perhaps even a release for the impotence that had roiled inside of her all day. Most of all, she wanted Jack without doubt, without the world intruding. In these moments, with her legs wrapped about him, embracing him tightly, she could protect him from the demons in his soul, from the desperation he'd let her glimpse tonight, desperation she hadn't known was there. The knowledge of such things increased her ecstasy. Paradise was within reach, peace was within reach.

She raised her hips, feeling his own hips grind against hers, the tempo of Jack's rhythm speeding towards completion, the pressure growing in his body, his muscled arms trembling as they held his weight, and knew his crisis would soon be upon him. Her own release neared, so very close she thought she'd scream from the wanting of it. Then they were there together, Jack's climax thundering deep inside her, pulsing in waves, releasing the most intimate of tides at the shore of her womb. This was completion.

They lay still, letting their breathing return to normal, their excited hearts regain their usual pace. Dulci relished the feel of Jack's head at her shoulder, his hand lying quiet on her stomach. Something intangible marked tonight. Their love-making had taken on a different cast, driven by something she couldn't name yet.

After a while, Jack rose and adjusted his clothing. He reached down to help her up and straighten her skirts. The desperation she thought she'd viewed in his eyes was effectively driven back. His eyes, his face, held a look of firm resolve as if something had been decided and there was no going back.

His teasing smile was on his lips. But his voice was soft, a near-whisper full of sincerity. 'This will definitely be more memorable than a conversation about hydrangeas and roses.'

At the intimate sound of his voice, something warm blossomed in the feminine core of her. She felt complete, wrapped in the shared memory of their passion conjured up by his voice. She was well and thoroughly seduced. But it was more than seduction. What she felt for Jack in that moment was far beyond the abilities of lust to sustain. *She loved him.* The realisation nearly brought her to her knees. All her defences, logic and hard cold reality, had failed to protect her. Against her better intentions, she'd fallen in love with the most unlikely of candidates for her heart: a man who would not give her his.

'You're trembling, Dulci. Don't worry, you're safe now.' Jack lifted her hand to his lips and pressed a kiss upon it, his eyes holding hers with a million unspoken messages tumbling in them. That was when Dulci understood; Jack thought he was going to die.

Chapter Eleven

It was empirically true that one never feels more alive than when faced with imminent mortality. Jack dressed in preparation for the opening negotiations, life surging through him, his senses imbued with a sharper, more vital quality. Jack worked a gold cuff into place, his eyes moving outside past the heavy curtains drawn back to let in the morning light.

The sun shone brilliantly. It was going to be a nice day in spite of the fact that nice things weren't going to happen. It was hard to believe anything bad could happen on sunny days. Hard to believe anyone could die on a sunny day. Those sorts of things ought to be reserved for rainy, gloomy days.

Jack reached for the second cuff link, remembering. He'd believed such fantasy as a child. Growing up just outside Manchester, there were plenty of grey days and in his house there'd been plenty of bad things that happened on them. Sunshine had meant freedom.

Nothing bad happened on sunny days. Sunshine meant running in the meadows and fishing in the rivers with Brandon, perfect days in an imperfect life.

Satisfied with his cuffs, Jack reached for a long strip of white linen and wound it around his neck, beginning the laborious process of tying a cravat. He'd dreamed of her last night, not surprising considering the circumstances and their rather torrid farewell.

Even now in the morning light, Dulci haunted him. He could not name why or how the endless wanting of her had started, but he craved her with the intensity of an opium addict. After the madness at Christmas he'd taken the necessary precautions. He'd tried long absences. He'd tried other women. All to no avail. His methods only seemed to increase the craving and he'd ended up right back where he'd started from.

And why not? Dulci was a rare treasure to be appreciated for far more than her fairy-tale princess beauty: the dark hair, the pale skin and cherry lips. He was drawn to her wildness, to the substance of her. Perhaps he was drawn to her because she was like him. He might not know her favourite colour, or know the name of her dressmaker or any of the mundane little facts that besotted fools who imagine themselves in love know about their beloved. But he knew her elementally. He knew what drove her wildness.

She was like him in all the ways that mattered. She *knew* him. She knew his family home, an awkward cold place devoid of familial love. She knew stories about him growing up. And she still cared for him, although he was playing fast and loose with that affection.

Jack tied a firm knot at his throat with a strong jerk of his hands. She knew him and he knew her, perhaps not in the traditional way people knew each other in London society, but in a way that spoke to the core of him. He might still be attempting to name this depth of feeling Dulci invoked in him, but he knew with a certainty that he was willing to die to save her. If Ortiz harmed her, a light would go out of the world, and Jack knew a part of himself would go out of the world with it. As long as one of the two survived... If given the choice, Jack preferred it be Dulci.

He strapped on an arm sheath and slid a small dagger into it. He leaned down and slid another knife into his boot. Ortiz was coming. Jack just hoped he had guessed correctly and Ortiz was coming for him. He would be ready. He had no intention of dying simply because Ortiz meant him to. Still, he'd played this game long enough to know death came in many forms: a hired thug on the street, a discreet poison in a glass. Some attempts could be thwarted with a quick blade. Other attempts could not.

Jack reached into his dresser drawer and rooted beneath a pile of cravats until he found what he wanted: travelling papers and a packet of money. He faced himself in the mirror, slipping his arms into his jacket of blue superfine.

He studied the reflection, deliberately forcing his mind to slow and focus, reviewing. He'd taken all the precautions he could. He'd left Dulci in her home, surrounded by the finest bodyguards the Foreign Office could provide. He'd armed himself for a physical attack. He had money and papers in case he had to flee, a ruby ring on his little finger and a matching stick pin in his cravat to pawn. If it came to it, he could sell the buttons on his coat one by one. He was an expert when it came to survival.

Satisfied that he'd taken all measures possible to ensure Dulci's safety and his own survival, Jack grabbed up the ornate walking stick from the stand by the door and strode confidently out into the morning to face life or death, come what may, with only one regret. He knew men who had died with more.

There were no regrets, only choices, Dulci reminded herself forcefully, struggling to concentrate on the arte-facts spread out before her. She'd set up a temporary workshop in an old greenhouse at the back of the garden while she waited for new cases to arrive and the windows to be repaired. But her energy was divided between the items spread before her and the items on her mind—the shocking revelations of the night before.

Jack was worried, so worried he'd attempted to draw Ortiz's fire and divert attention from her. She was not sure how she felt about that. She was used to fighting her own battles, but never had she faced a battle like this. This was not a battle over social acceptance, but about life and death. She was out of her depth when it came to secret assassins and hidden maps.

She'd spent a restless night and a restless morning

trying to put the image of Jack out of her mind without success. The guards placed around the house had told her the negotiations started today.

Jack would be there by now, seated at the long table with other men, Calisto Ortiz across from him just a few feet away, close enough to strike with a dagger if Ortiz didn't mind the publicity. Why should he if he had immunity and the argument of honour on his side? Not that it was any better assuming Ortiz would refrain from a public spilling of blood. Covert activity was far worse, where even the simplest cup of tea became a weapon in an expert's hands. One sip and Jack would be gone, taken from her, sacrificed for her, just when she'd discovered she loved him.

She loved Jack. The realisation was so fresh, so new, she hardly knew what to make of it. But she did know where to start and that was with the question: Did she dare give in to it? She wasn't exactly sure she had a choice. Could you control whom you loved? But assuming she did have a choice, Dulci wasn't sure she could afford to love Jack. In the end, it might cost more of herself than she was willing to give. She would not tolerate living on the periphery of his world, even if that was the only way she could have him.

There were terrible consequences to loving Jack, she was beginning to realise with a new level of clarity. He might die. She might have to give him up and not act on her affections for the sake of saving her own soul. Either way, she'd be left alone with her love—alone and apart from Jack.

Dulci's pen slipped, smearing ink on the carefully written card. At this rate she wouldn't get any work done. Dulci flopped down into an old wicker chair that had been left or forgot when the greenhouse had been abandoned. A little cloud of dust puffed up from the faded cushions and she sneezed. Damn. She allowed herself the luxury of swearing. Would nothing go right today? Even the simple act of sitting down irritated her.

It was all Jack's fault. She'd never asked him to protect her, never asked him to stand between her and Calisto Ortiz. He did not owe her anything. But he'd stood her champion none the less and it had complicated things immensely. The thought she didn't want to think surfaced, unable to be contained by denial and anger— why had Jack done it? Had he done it out of fraternal affection for Brandon? Because Brandon would want him to protect her in his absence? Or maybe this wasn't about Brandon at all, but because there was something more between the two of them? Was it possible that he might reciprocate the intensity of feeling she carried towards him?

Dulci picked at a loose seam on the pillow. She wondered if it had ever been just sex for her, no matter what logical justifications she applied. That day in the artefact room, she'd trusted Jack with her body and he'd not let her down. Even now, he was protecting her body with his distance, his bodyguards, his attempt to direct Ortiz away from her. Jack had never pretended to offer more than a few nights of unconditional pleasure.

Yet if she knew one thing about men, it was that they

protected what they loved. Was it possible that, against the odds, Jack had fallen in love with her? Had he slipped into it just as she had? If so, what did they do now? Anything? Nothing? Was it possible to be in love and do nothing? Someone would have to be brave enough to make the first move, declare their feelings and weather whatever storm came.

'Lady Dulcinea!' One of the bodyguards burst into the greenhouse, the door banging behind him. 'There's news from the negotiations.' Ah, even love would have to give way in the wake of the empire's needs. Jack wasn't even here and she was being interrupted, her thoughts called away from their feminine daydreams to Jack's world.

The man was breathless and the look on his face was not one of excitement. 'What has happened?' Dulci's anxiety rose.

'Viscount Wainsbridge has been accused of framing Señor Ortiz in regard to presenting a forged map of boundaries.'

'It's not true,' Dulci said in consternation. The incredible claim was wildly untrue; a bigger lie she could not imagine, especially when the exact opposite was true. 'Who accuses him of such a thing?' She was on her feet, pacing. She had to do something, take some action. Jack would need her.

'Señor Ortiz himself.'

Ah, like the witch trials of old where only the afflicted was able to bear testimony against the accused. A cold thought indeed.

* * *

Calisto Ortiz was inordinately pleased with himself. This plan had hatched itself flawlessly. The negotiations had opened and the British had asked he be excused from the negotiations. They had concerns about his 'objectivity', that he was associated with the murder of an importer who'd carried cargo from Venezuela and had been in possession of a certain map. That map had fallen into the hands of a British citizen and been the source of an attempted burglary of the citizen's home. Since the map was a forgery, it appeared Señor Ortiz had a hidden agenda to swindle land from the British government. It would be best to excuse him due to a conflict of interest.

It had been nicely said, but Vargas had clearly understood the message. The old diplomat had sputtered, voicing embarrassed protests to save face. Then he'd jumped in, adding to Vargas's protests. He'd merely said, 'I've been set up by Viscount Wainsbridge, who is in possession of the map and who has a personal grudge against me over a woman. It seems to me that if I were trying to pass off a map I would have the map in my possession. Yet it is Wainsbridge who "found" the map, not in my quarters, I might add. In fact, not once has the map been in my possession since arriving on English soil.'

His claims were audacious, but the bigger the lie, the more easily believed. He didn't have to have anyone believe him. He needed only to cast enough doubt to cloud the discussion. He watched Gladstone spear Wainsbridge with a look of disgust. Ah, good, a potential ally then. Wainsbridge showed no emotion, managing to look cool, as if people levelled charges of this magnitude against him daily. For all Ortiz knew, maybe they did.

Señor Vargas turned to Ortiz. 'You swear this is the truth?'

Vargas was so damned honourable he couldn't conceive of dishonour in anyone. Ortiz stifled a smile and manufactured a look of chagrin. He laid his next layer of argument, the layer meant to distract and confuse. 'I swear this is the truth. I would encourage you, *señor*, to ask yourself why would Britain want to put a forgery into play that shows them losing land? It is to start a war.' There was a general outcry at the table. Ortiz raised a hand for silence.

'I posit Britain wants to use the false map as a chance to whip up public support for a war in which Britain is fighting to take back what Venezuela has "cheated" them out of. It would be no difficult feat for Britain, an empire with an enormous army at its disposal, to defeat Venezuela and in the end grab *more* land. These talks are merely a prelude to war. We've been called here to be straw men. These talks mean nothing. Britain is using them for a larger, more sinister purpose and Viscount Wainsbridge is at the heart of it.'

So this was how it was going to happen. Not with a knife in the alley or poison in the tea, at least not yet. Jack watched Ortiz spin his case with steely eyes. There would be discrediting first, the maligning of a reputation, the casting of doubt until people might believe with enough certainty that he'd commit suicide over the shame of it. Of course, it wouldn't truly be a suicide. That would be when Ortiz would arrange a violent end and his body would float up from the Thames a few days later. People would whisper knowingly behind their fans that he'd had no choice really, disgraced as he was, and what could be expected when one came from such lowly antecedents, a squire's son after all?

The difficulty came in making his case. He could not say Britain had advance warning that a map might exist without exposing the intelligence network that had brought the news. He could not say Ortiz had gone to the warehouse without exposing that he'd followed Ortiz and spied on him. There was only one piece of evidence he could legitimately draw on.

Jack steepled his hands. 'Your claims are outrageous. There is no interest in starting a war with Venezuela. Your scenario is intriguing, but it does not account for the testimony we have from the one burglar who says he was paid, by you, Señor Ortiz, to retrieve a map from Lady Dulcinea's residence.'

Ortiz shook his head sadly. 'That was poor judgement on my part. I was so distraught over the news of such a map and Señor Vasquez's death. I had just heard and I was desperate to preserve my reputation. I acted hastily and foolishly. I thought if I could get the map, I could destroy it and none of this nastiness would materialise.'

'How did you know the map would be at Lady Dulcinea's?' The question seemed to flummox Ortiz for a moment before his eyes narrowed and his mouth quirked into a smirk.

'Perhaps I should ask you the same? How did you happen to be there?'

'You've been suspected from the start,' Jack growled, his anger overriding his sang-froid.

'Lying in wait for me? No doubt it's because you knew I'd come, that I'd have no choice in order to save my reputation.' Ortiz rose from his seat, his hands braced on the table. 'You've had me framed from the start, since the first night you tried to make a fool of me at the ball, all because Lady Dulcinea was taken with me, and not you.'

Gladstone coughed furiously at the far end of the table.

'I prefer to have Lady Dulcinea, who is nothing but an innocent bystander in this, left out of the discussion.' Jack rose to meet Ortiz across the table, all his instincts firing: protect, protect, protect. Protect Dulci. Protect the crown.

Gladstone rose and cleared his throat. 'Gentleman, there must be a suitable resolution to this misunderstanding. Let us take a brief recess to sort this out. Wainsbridge, a word, please?'

Jack shut the door of a small blue salon behind him. The place was quiet and private, a chance to talk. 'The man is talking nonsense,' Jack declared the moment they were alone.

'Is he? How do we prove that?' Gladstone shook his head and paced the floor. 'Can we produce the map?'

'Yes, I can get it,' Jack said evasively. If Gladstone did not leap to his defence, then Gladstone could not be trusted. The man should have done more for him back there besides cough in disbelief. 'What good will that do? It will only prove I am in possession of a map that contains boundaries unlike the ones on the Humboldt map.'

'Hmm. That would only make you look guiltier, I suppose.' Gladstone stopped to fiddle with the top on a crystal decanter. 'Wainsbridge, did you plant the map? It would have been ingenious. You hear the king and I mention the potential for the map's existence and then you decide to make that potential reality.'

Jack whirled on Gladstone incredulously. 'You heard the king, he said he needed me to stop a war, not start one.'

Gladstone shrugged. 'There's more glory in war than in peace, Jack, and you're a man who hungers for adventure.'

'I did not plant the map. Everything happened as our intelligence said—the map was hidden in Vasquez's cargo. It was a stroke of luck that Dulci happened to have it. Otherwise, the cargo would have disappeared into London.'

Gladstone nodded, cringing a bit at his easy use of Dulci's first name. 'You understand I had to ask.'

Jack met his gaze evenly. 'I understand that you're willing to sacrifice me for the sake of these negotiations.' He saw what Gladstone wanted. Gladstone wanted him to gracefully bow out of the negotiations, but that wouldn't stop the rumours circulating as to why he'd left. Such a gesture wouldn't stop Ortiz's tongue from wagging. Worst of all, if he bowed out, then Ortiz would be entirely vindicated while he would be all but ruined, the banner of scandal firmly affixed above his head for the rest of his life: the man who tried to start a war with a lie.

'I won't do it, Gladstone.' He had worked too hard to lose it all like this. It was one thing to want to give it up. It was another to be stripped of it in shame. What would Dulci think of him? He could not stand to lose her so soon after realising what she meant to him. But he'd rather give her up to protect her from his scandal than drag her down with him.

Gladstone moved towards the door, his hand hovering over the knob. 'There are a lot of ways to serve your country, Wainsbridge. Consider this yours.'

'No,' Jack said defiantly. 'I will go to the king. I will prove the map is a fraud, drawn up at the behest of Calisto Ortiz.'

Gladstone gave a hoarse laugh. 'How will you do that? You'd have to go all the way to Guiana. You'd have to find the map-maker and wring a confession from him. You'd have to sail down the river and prove its course runs counter to the drawing.'

'Then that is what I'll do,' Jack said with grim determination. Hercules had his twelve labours, Jack had his.

Chapter Twelve

A more regal king would have sided with Gladstone and, with a show of great reluctance, washed his hands of Jack Hanley, the first Viscount Wainsbridge, a man of no account when compared to the generations of service provided by Gladstone's family. There was no one, no great family or genealogical history to offend by doing so. But William IV was of a more plebian mind. He defined his rule by his support of reform, by lessening the gap between the entitlements of gentlemen and the entitlements of the common man. As such, he felt it unnecessary to sacrifice Jack for the good of the order.

William fixed his gaze on the two men sitting before him shortly after midnight. 'This is unbecoming of you, Gladstone. I am disappointed you have not championed Wainsbridge publicly. The Venezuelans must not suspect we can be so easily divided and conquered. If they think we will break ranks over this, they may think we are easily manipulated on other issues as well.'

'I had to be sure of Wainsbridge's actions, your Majesty.' Gladstone went red in the face.

William offered him a look of disbelief. 'An Englishman does not need to doubt another Englishman. What was there to be sure of? We do not make a practice of disgracing viscounts. By disgracing Wainsbridge, you disgrace me and my good judgement.'

Jack disliked having to involve the king, but when faced with utter ruination, he needed an advocate. Left to Gladstone's mercy, he'd have ended up under house arrest and no recourse. It was a petty victory to see Gladstone red as a rooster, but a victory none the less and Jack would take it.

'Your Majesty, I appreciate your support,' Jack began humbly. 'However, there is still the issue of the map. It is not an accurate representation of landownership on the border. Until a definite, first-hand study of the border can be made, my greater fear is that this map is only the first. We make ourselves weak if we haven't the proof to defend ourselves. Venezuela will come again. There will be others like Ortiz, even if we scotch this particular effort. Humboldt's map is only a suggestion. He did not explore the Essequibo region.'

William looked thoughtful, a hand caressing his soft double chin in contemplation. 'I see your point. Undefended borders have historically been problems for all empires. What do you suggest, Wainsbridge?'

Jack leaned forwards in his excitement, careful with his words. 'I suggest we map the area immediately.'

'And who should do the mapping? Do you have anyone

in mind?' A glimmer of a smile played on William's lips as if he understood the direction of Jack's thoughts.

'Robert Schomburgk, with whom I worked on the Anegada exploration, is already over there, but I would willingly offer myself to work in tandem with him, although I would gladly do it alone if he is too busy. This must be done in a timely fashion.'

'Brilliant!' William slapped his leg jovially. 'I like how you think, Wainsbridge. You're a man of action.' He turned sharp eyes on Gladstone. 'This is the perfect solution, the perfect proof. Do you see it, Gladstone?' William winked at Jack. 'Killing two birds with one stone, eh?'

Jack nodded, elation and relief filling him simultaneously after the stress of the afternoon. The map would serve two purposes. First, it would define the currently ambiguous borders of ownership between Venezuela and British Guiana, preventing future contentions. Second, it would absolve him of Ortiz's flimsy claim that he wanted to start a war. No one would create one map and then deliberately draw up another, contradictory one.

He would create an honest map that showed no need to quibble over territory because Britain already possessed it rightfully. Now, the burden of initiating hostilities would fall to the Venezuelans. *They* would be the invaders, not the British. If there was a war, Britain would not start it. And he would be clear in the process, his reputation intact. He would not be the man who betrayed Britain by giving away land. In the process, if he happened to find the man who'd been paid to draw